THE
BIRNEY
DAY SCHOOL

THE
BIRNEY
DAY SCHOOL

A Novel

By Philip Hall

WordsWorth Publishing
Cody, Wyoming

ISBN 978-1-7334897-9-9
First edition paperback

Cover photo: *View of Birney, Montana with school in background.* Huffman, L. A. (Laton Alton), 1854-1931, Birney, Montana (Between 1879-1930). Montana History Portal, accessed 28/10/2025, https://www.mtmemory.org/nodes/view/72268

Published by WordsWorth
Cody, Wyoming
www.wordsworthpublishing.com

CONTENTS

CHAPTER ONE

The Frisbee Catcher

Many life-altering events are happenstances. Some happenstances are auspicious. Others are the precursors of pain, suffering, and disaster, and they occur simply because we were at a certain place at a particular time. Such is the nature of life, always uncertain, occasionally precarious, but sometimes auspicious.

"Children, don't play on the swings," a woman called out. "You'll wake the man sleeping in the tent." My eyes snapped open. What were children doing out there? Last evening the country schoolhouse had looked abandoned, promising solace to a weary traveler. Believing it, I pitched my tent on the playground's grass. And how did the woman know only one man was sleeping in the tent? Had she looked in on me?

Quickly pulling on my pants, I slipped on a shirt and emerged into the bright light of the sun, already high above the horizon. The playground was full of children—Indian children. They were paired off in two lines, playing some type of game. A boy, who looked to be about twelve years old, whipped his arm and out shot a frisbee. The red disk skimmed just above the ground and sped toward the opposing team. With one last display of power, it made a quick, steep climb, and soared over the heads and above the outstretched arms of the waiting children. The frisbee rose to its apex and hung suspended in space. Glistening in the sun, the flimsy piece of plastic held gravity in abeyance as if it possessed an unearthly power. But its moment of glory, like most triumphs, was fleeting. It began to flutter. A stall was imminent. The frisbee was about to plummet to earth.

Out of the corner of my eye, I saw a young, jean-clad Indian woman running with space-consuming strides as she wove in and out of the children. As she neared the frisbee, the woman leaped free from the bounds of the earth and soared into the air. Stretching every fiber of her body to its limit, she reached one hand high into the air and snatched the frisbee right out of the sky. What a catch!

To the cheers of her young admirers, the frisbee catcher came back to earth, nearly landing at my feet. The young woman took a searching look at me. As I nodded my head to apologize for trespassing, she scrutinized me, apparently thinking about whether to accept my repentance. Slowly, my eyes wandered back toward hers, but the woman interrupted the journey short of its destination. "Go through that door," she said, gesturing to a basement stairwell. "On the far side of the lunchroom there are stairs. The door to the left of the stairs opens to the bathrooms. You are welcome to use it." Turning, she threw the frisbee to a child in the other line, and the game resumed.

I was halfway to the basement door when a soft whistle sounded behind me. It was the frisbee catcher. She was calling me back for more instructions. "Then find Maggie. She needs help today." Becoming stern, the young woman continued. "Call her Mrs. Fighting Bear. Don't offer to shake her hand and do not look directly into her eyes. You know, show respect. She's an elder."

The basement was a lunchroom. To the left, there were three rows of lunch tables. To the right, a large Dutch window opened into an efficient-looking kitchen. A few feet farther down the wall was a similarly shaped but smaller window. Ahead, stairs led up to the classrooms. Opening the door to the left of the stairs led me to the bathrooms. The first one was marked GIRLS. The second was labeled BOYS.

I was washing my hands when, overhead, a throng of children thundered up the stairs to their classrooms. When silence prevailed, I cautiously opened the door to the lunchroom, peered out, and looked into the face of an elderly Indian woman. She was firmly planted between me and the basement door and appeared to be as immovable as a New England Patriot linebacker. The woman had a broad face, one that could have accommodated a smile, but didn't.

She glared at me with icicle eyes.

As instructed, I looked down at the floor and said, "Hello, Mrs. Fighting Bear. I was told to help you."

"I knowed that!" the old woman growled. "Sarah told me this mornin' that the Whiteman who pitched his tent on our playground would be my helper." Holding out a pail of hot, soapy water and a clean dishcloth, she barked, "Clean tables." Without waiting for a reply, she shuffled back into the kitchen.

After washing the tables, I carried the pail of dirty water into the kitchen. Mrs. Fighting Bear was standing at a chopping block, attacking a pile of carrots with a large, wicked-looking knife. With unnerving efficiency, she cleanly cut off each carrot's green top and sliced off the tip with a knife as sharp as a surgical scalpel. Holding out the pail, I asked, "Where should I dump this?" The cook nodded her head toward a drain sink in the corner.

After dumping the water, I turned around to find Mrs. Fighting Bear standing behind me with a mop bucket of hot water and a mop. "Mop the lunchroom floor," she directed.

When the floor was mopped and the water dumped down the drain sink, Mrs. Fighting Bear pointed toward a stack of metal trays. Gesturing toward a little table on the lunchroom side of the large Dutch window, she said, "Set 'em there, and set out forks, knives, and spoons. Don't forget napkins!"

The metal trays, the tray of cutlery, and napkins were no sooner set out than children came pouring down the stairs like a wall of water breaching a dam. They lined up at the Dutch window and waited for their lunch. Mrs. Fighting Bear tied an apron around my waist and placed me behind a huge bowl of mashed potatoes. Taking a position immediately to my left, she placed a hamburger on the tray each student presented. As the children passed by me, I dished out a scoop of mashed potatoes. When everyone had been served, the cook put her bear-claw hand on my back and guided me to the small Dutch window. There, the children handed me their dirty trays. I scraped whatever was left on trays—used bubble gum and snotty napkins—into a galvanized trash can. I turned the task into a mindless routine. With unfocused eyes, I grabbed each proffered tray, put the cutlery into a metal tub of soapy water, stacked the tray, and reached for the next one. However, this one was anchored. Looking up, I saw that the tray was firmly held by fingers that were delicate yet strong. Following the fingers, I looked into dark-brown eyes that twinkled with intelligence, laughed with mischievousness, and mesmerized me.

"You do good work," the frisbee catcher commented as she flashed a self-satisfied grin. Before I could formulate a reply, she walked away.

When the trays had been collected and stacked, Mrs. Fighting Bear assigned me my next task—washing the cutlery, the trays, and the cooking pots. When that was done, she told me to wipe the tables and mop the floor. The dirty water in the mop bucket was no sooner poured down the drain sink than Mrs. Fighting Bear shuffled up with another pail of hot, soapy water and a clean dishcloth. Pointing to the pantry, she growled, "Wash the shelves. Get 'em real clean!"

As I worked, my thoughts turned to the frisbee catcher. She could not be more than twenty-four years old, yet she clearly was the hub around which everything and everyone at the school revolved. Why had the young woman conned me into assisting Mrs. Fighting Bear? Obviously, her cook needed a helper that morning, but I fantasized there was another reason.

It was three o'clock when the last pantry shelf was cleaned and its items restored to their rightful place. I stepped out of the pantry and approached Mrs. Fighting Bear, who was tidying up the kitchen. "What's next? I asked.

"You go now," she replied.

That was it? No 'Thank you' or even an appreciative nod. Simply, 'You go now!'

Well, I was ready to go. The price for trespassing onto the school yard last evening had been exorbitant. I wasted no time breaching the basement door and starting toward my tent, which was still pitched on the school's playground.

I was only four steps out of the door when a soft whistle came from the window above me. Turning and looking up, I saw it was the frisbee catcher. "Cross the bridge and head east," she said. "When you come to a fork in the road, turn left, back the way you came last evening. Go twenty yards down the road and you'll see a lightly used road coming in on the right. It'll take you up Poker Jim Creek. The road dead-ends in less than a mile. Camp there. Then come tomorrow morning to help Mrs. Fighting Bear."

How did the woman know the route I had taken to reach the Birney Day School? According to the map, four roads came together within a mile of the school. I could have arrived at the school via any one of the four. But how she knew my route to the school was not the uppermost thing in my mind. The uppermost thing was how to politely but firmly say, 'No! No thanks. I'll be moving on.'

A harsh "No" started deep in my chest and worked its way up my throat. Perceiving it, the frisbee catcher put a finger to her lips and shook her head in disapproval. "Think of the children," she said.

"The children?"

"Yes, the children. Maggie can't possibly get the children's lunch prepared and served without your help."

"Well, okay. I will help her."

"Good. Be here by nine-thirty."

Looking up, I expected to bask in the warmth of the frisbee catcher's appreciative smile, but she was gone.

CHAPTER TWO

Playing out My Hand

"You've got to know when to hold 'em; know when to fold 'em. Every hand's a winner, and every hand's a loser."

Don Schlitz's song, The Gambler, *recorded by Kenny Rogers*

The "road" to Poker Jim Creek was nothing more than ruts worn into the prairie. But then Poker Jim Creek wasn't really a creek. It was a bone-dry wash in the bottom of a narrow gulch carved out by an occasional cloudburst. When I had driven a little more than a half mile, the hills pinched against the creek and the road ended. A large cottonwood tree invited me to pitch my tent under its consoling branches. To the immediate south, east, and north, steep hills blocked the wind, making the campsite well-sheltered. Across the creek, the yellow leaves of a cluster of ash trees fluttered in the breeze, hinting that fall would soon come calling. From high up in the cottonwood tree, a magpie scolded me for intruding into its domain.

As the sun slid toward the western horizon, I sat on the tailgate of my pickup, ate sardines out of a can, and listened to the radio. It was news time. The announcer reported that Henry Kissinger was in Paris holding peace talks with the North Vietnamese. A mule deer came out of a side draw to seek the green grass that grew in the bottom of the gulch. Finding a new and unfamiliar object in her way, the doe circled around my pickup, taking an inconvenient but safer route. With every step, she cast her eyes about, put her nose to the wind, twisted her ears this way, and proceeded cautiously. "I suppose you wonder why I'm here," I softly said to the deer. "Well, I've been dealt a hand, and I'm going to stay around long enough to see how it plays out."

Tuesday morning, I arrived at the school at nine-thirty. The children were out for recess, but the frisbee catcher was not with them. Instead of playing, the children wandered aimlessly. The older girls huddled by themselves, buzzing about something apparently confidential. If their whispers and darting eyes could be believed, the topic was juicy. The older boys picked up stones and, without announcing it, found themselves competing to see who could throw a rock the farthest. The younger boys played tag, but their game did not last long before dissension set in and broke it up. Finding nothing else to do, a group of little girls ambled toward the swings.

In the kitchen, Mrs. Fighting Bear was putting a big sack of potatoes on her worktable. "Good morning," I said cheerfully, seizing upon the possibility of getting the day started on a pleasant note. Grunting something that seemed like it might be a greeting, she pointed at a potato peeler and bobbed her head toward a pile of potatoes. As my hand reached for the first potato, the matron of the ladle stomped her foot.

"Wash hands!" she scolded.

While I peeled potatoes, three teachers came down for their morning coffee break while their colleague, the day's designated recess supervisor, monitored the students. Mrs. Fighting Bear poured herself a cup of coffee. She took it into the lunchroom, sat a table directly behind the teachers, and listened to their every word.

The rest of the morning's tasks were the same as the ones the day before — wash and wipe the tables, mop the floor, and set out the trays and cutlery. The tasks were finished by eleven. As I looked around to see what needed to be done next, Mrs. Fighting Bear came out of the kitchen with a tray of food. "Eat," she said, holding out the tray.

I had just sat down to eat when an Indian man came through the basement door and disappeared into the kitchen. He soon emerged with a tray of food and came straight to the lunchroom table where I was sitting. In height, the man was a few inches short of average and sported a modest paunch that hung comfortably over his plate-sized belt buckle. On his head sat a six-beaver Stetson that, many years ago, had been white and had cost a pretty penny. The hat was now well-weathered and spotted with sweat stains, dabs of dried blood, drops of oil, and dirt. He wore dark-brown cowboy boots that in their long life had seen much mud and little polish. Setting his tray on the table and taking seat across the table from me, he said, "Name's Joe. Joe Fightin' Bear. I try to keep the roof of the school from fallin' in." While introducing himself, Mr. Fighting Bear looked me over from head to toe with eyes that asked, "And who are you, and what in the hell are you doing in my school?"

Standing up and holding out my hand, I said, "Glad to meet you, Mr. Fighting Bear," Seemingly startled by my gesture of friendship, he hesitated momentarily and then reluctantly extended a meaty paw. Ignoring his less-than-welcoming body language, I warmly said, "My name's Wagner, Jonathan Wagner. I've been recruited to help the cook for a few days. She must be your wife."

"Ya mean the old bat who can curdle milk with one look!" As a smirk flashed on his face, he continued. "Yup, I claim her. But she's not the porcupine that she seems, leastways not if she likes ya."

"Oh," I replied, unconsciously casting a concerned look toward the kitchen.

"No worry," he said. "She thinks your hair is too short to make a proper scalp, eh?"

We ate in silence for a while. But having driven halfway across the country and gone for days with little human contact, I was eager for conversation. To get the ball rolling, I resorted to the time-honored safe topic, the weather, "Tell me, Mr. Fighting Bear, are all days in Montana as perfect as this one?"

"Not all of 'em. There are days in the summer when the thermometer climbs above a hundred and the wind blows hot, dryin' a man out like an old hide. You'd think the country was either gonna dry up and blow away or burn up. In the winter, it can get bone-chillin' cold. Twenty below zero is right common, and thirty below sometimes happens. Some winters we get lots of snow. Take the winter of forty-nine. In January that year, a blizzard came across the Northern Plains that shut everything down for a month. Nobody and nothin' moved. Thousands of cattle died. But in the fall we go for day after day just like today," he said, gesturing toward the screen door and the sixty-five-degree day with a wisp of a breeze and a cloudless, deep-blue sky. "I use to guide rich folks on hunts up in the Bighorns in the fall. The country was beautiful, aspen all golden and the tops of the mountains white with a dustin' of new snow." Then, as if Mr. Fighting Bear's reminiscing encountered a bad memory, his eyes refocused. "But some of the customers thought my name was Festus. It was fetch this and get me that. I quit, eh? By askin' around, I landed a job workin' for a big operator northwest of Miles City. It was good work. The rancher ran cattle like it was the eighteen hundreds. We put the cows out to pasture durin' the summer. After the calves were sold in October, we trailed the cows into the Missouri River breaks where they went all winner without a spear of hay. But the rancher paid like it was the old times—forty bucks a month, room an' board, and all the broncs ya wanted to ride. One Saturday night, I went into Miles City to a dance, and there I met Maggie. We started seein' each other every weekend. Before long, we was hitched. We moved into a place down here along The Tongue River to be near her folks and . . ."

And then the children came pouring down the stairs with a wave of energy that put everyone on notice. Mrs. Fighting Bear gestured for me to come to the kitchen's Dutch window and tasked me with spooning cooked carrots onto the students' trays.

After the children had eaten lunch and gone out for noon recess, I mopped the lunchroom floor while Mrs. Fighting Bear turned on the oven and started preparing something that needed baking. The children, three of the four teachers, Mr. Fighting Bear, and the frisbee catcher were outside enjoying the beautiful day. Noon recess had gone on for thirty minutes, when Mrs. Johnson, the teacher of the first/second grade room, came clomping down the stairs. She goose-stepped across the lunchroom to the basement door. Standing with the rigidity of a prison guard, she surveyed the playground. Neither the children nor any of the adults saw her, and that set Mrs. Johnson's right foot tapping with increasing agitation. A red sheen rose at the base of her neck and crept upward. When the redness reached Mrs. Johnson's ears, she let out a loud, air-piercing screech. "Recess is over," she screamed. "Now get in here!"

As the children entered the school, I stood by the door leaning on the mop handle, gape-mouthed at Mrs. Johnson's uncalled-for outburst. When the frisbee catcher passed by me, she noticed my astonishment. Giving me a reassuring pat on my shoulder, she said, "Joe's waiting for you outside."

Mr. Fighting Bear was sitting on the ground, propped against the school's foundation. Seeing me, he snuffed out his cigarette under the heel of his boot and stood up. With a come-along wave of his arm, he walked toward an old Chevy pickup loaded with cardboard boxes that rose two feet above the cab's roof and were held in place by a half-inch rope that zig-zagged across the load from front to back. Seeing the quizzical look on my face, he said, "School supplies and Uncle Sam's commodities. I took everything the BIA Office in Billings would give me. Help me unload this stuff."

After half of the boxes were carried into the school, Mr. Fighting Bear said that it was time for a break. As we sat down along the school's south-facing foundation to soak up the sun's warmth, he reached into his shirt pocket for a sack of Bull Durham and an orange-colored pad of cigarette papers from which he extracted a flimsy, almost transparent paper. Holding the delicate paper in his left hand, he carefully shook the sack of Bull Durham, depositing a thin line of tobacco onto the paper. Using his thick index finger, Mr. Fighting Bear spread the flakes evenly from one end of the paper to the other. Seeing a microscopic insufficiency, he gently shook the sack of Bull Durham and smiled as a few more flakes of tobacco floated down. Satisfied, he curled the paper around the tobacco, caressed the edge with his tongue and, with the utmost tenderness, sealed the rolled paper. He inspected the finished product, nodded his head in approval, and put a match to his artistry. Nicotine soon coursed through his blood. He was content.

"Mr. Fighting Bear, what can you tell me about this school?" I asked, more to break the silence than out of interest.

"It wasn't the first school on the rez. The first school was the mission school in Ashland. I was told it got going around eighteen eighty-four. A couple of years later, another school was started in Lame Deer. It wasn't much, just a one-room log buildin' barely big enough to hold a few kids and a teacher. Then in nineteen ought four, the Indian Department built a boardin' school at Busby. The boardin' school was a bad place. When the kids came in the fall for the start of school, they were stripped of their clothes and dipped like sheep in a vat of hot-as-hell water with a little kerosene. To make sure the hot water and the kerosene killed all the vermin the teachers feared the kids was carrin', the teachers pushed the kid's head under the water a couple of times. The clothes the kids' mothers had made for them were burned, and the kids were dressed in Whiteman's clothes. The boys' long hair, their sign of manliness, was chopped off. The girls' hair was braided. If a kid was caught talkin' Cheyenne, his mouth was washed out with soap. The teachers saw their job as makin' Indian kids into white kids, and they worked real hard at it. Most of the time, a bunch of kids were missin' from the boardin' school. They snuck out of the dorm as soon as it got dark and caught a ride with anyone goin' in the direction of their home. An' if no one was goin' toward their home, the kids, some of 'em wee little things, walked up to ten miles to get home.

"Wow! You're right. That boarding school sounds like it was a horrible place."

"It sure was, and that is why every mornin' the headmaster gave a list of the missin' kids to the Indian police, and the police soon came callin'. But when the police got to the kid's house, most of the time nobody was home. If the parents happened to be home, they told the police they hadn't seen the kid for days. The police, bein' Indian themselves, knowed what was happenin'. Even if they saw a pair of little feet stickin' out from under a blanket, they went back to Busby and told the headmaster they couldn't find hide nor hair of the missin' kid. Things at the mission school in Ashland were pretty much the same. That's why in nineteen-ten they got a school going down here in Birney. It was got goin' by an old medicine man by the name of Young Bird because he didn't like how the kids were bein' treated at the government boardin' school or at the mission school. He said that Three Fingers had been to a white man's school and knew a lot. He could teach the kids right here. That's how the Birney Day School got goin'. That was before my time, but I have been told the kids were taught the regular school things, readin', writin', and figgerin'. But the best thing about the

Birney Day School was that bein' Indian was okay. The kids could talk Cheyenne, and Cheyenne ceremonies were held right here on the school grounds. Hearin' good things about the school, families moved down here so their kids could go to a school that taught them while honoring their culture. So, this little school got bigger. In about nineteen-forty or so, the Indian Department built us a new school, the one we are leaning against. They also built that house over there," Mr. Fighting Bear said, pointing to an abandoned two-story house about a hundred yards southeast of the school. It was for the unhitched teachers.

"For years, things at our little school went good. But in the last few years, lots of folks have moved to Lame Deer and Busby where they lean against the post office and look up and down the highway to see what might be comin' an' what might be goin'. There are not many kids left down here on the river. I don't know how many more years we can keep this school goin'." With that, he squashed out his cigarette, signaling it was time to get back to work.

As Mr. Fighting Bear and I carried the last two boxes into the school, Mrs. Fighting Bear pulled a pan of cinnamon rolls from the oven, scraped them onto a plate, and carried the plate to the lunchroom. The aroma of the fresh-baked rolls floated through the screen door; it traveled far and wide, and it traveled fast. Within minutes, the door opened and an elderly Indian woman entered. She deposited a sack of squash on the closest lunchroom table and proceeded to the table where cinnamon rolls and hot coffee waited. Another woman soon arrived. She put a sack of Montana-grown apples on the table and joined Maggie and the first woman. Before long, six elderly Indian women, including Mrs. Fighting Bear, were sitting at the table, eating cinnamon rolls, drinking black coffee laced with sugar, and jabbering like magpies while alternating between speaking in Cheyenne and speaking in English. When the women left, each carried away a sack of the very things Mr. Fighting Bear and I had just unloaded from the pickup—sugar, coffee, canned goods, and toilet paper.

When I arrived at the school Wednesday morning, the children were out for recess. The four teachers were in the lunchroom drinking coffee. Mrs. Fighting Bear was in her customary position at the table right behind them, peeling Montana-grown apples. As I breached the basement door, Mr. Fighting Bear came out of his workroom. Seeing me, he said, "Time for a smoke."

We stepped into the warm sunshine and took our stations along the school's south-facing foundation. On the playground, the frisbee catcher was organizing the children into games according to their ages, interests, and abilities. She was the only adult present, but managing the forty-eight children was no problem for her. The children hung on her every word.

"Sure is pretty," Mr. Fighting Bear commented as he got out the makings to roll a cigarette.

"What's pretty?" I asked.

"Sarah," he replied, irritated that he had to point out the obvious. We both looked again, as if we needed another surveillance to convince ourselves. "Ya know, don't ya, that white folk think the Indians have princesses and each tribe has its own Pocahontas. Well, they don't. But if the Northern Cheyenne had a princess, it'd sure enough be her."

"Tell me, Mr. Fighting Bear," I said, seizing on the opportunity to ask a question that had been on my mind for two days, "Does the princess have a prince?" Without looking at me, he shrugged his shoulders, which either meant, I'm not sure, or it's none of your business.

CHAPTER THREE

I Got Fired

By Thursday, being the cook's assistant had become routine, and it had become boring—peel potatoes, carrots, apples, or whatever; wash the lunchroom tables; mop the floor; set out the lunch trays and cutlery; eat lunch with Mr. Fighting Bear; serve the students; scrape trays; wash the cutlery, the trays, and the pots and pans; wipe the tables; and mop the basement floor. Whereas Mrs. Fighting Bear and I were not on the best of terms, we had what might be called a "working relationship." That is to say, we pretty much ignored each other as she went about preparing the noon lunch and I did the hygienic ritual.

I was mopping the lunchroom floor that morning when Sarah came down the stairs. "Hi," she said, walking to the edge of where the floor was freshly mopped. "You'll help Maggie tomorrow, won't you?"

"Yes. I will be her assistant one more day."

"Good," she replied and started to walk away.

I sent my voice chasing her, "Sarah."

"Yes, she replied, turning to look at me.

"Would you like to do something this evening?" Seeing a puzzled look come over her face, I quickly added, "Like go out to dinner?"

"A fancy place?"

"Yes, a fancy place!"

"A fancy place with linen tablecloths, cloth napkins, two forks, not only a water glass but also a wine glass, and, of course, romantically dim lighting?"

"Perfect!"

"I'd love to spend an evening like that with you, but there's one little problem,"

"What would that be?"

"The place I heard about that is fancy-like is a three-hour drive just to get there," she replied with a smirk. Before I could think of a salvaging response, Sarah went into the kitchen to talk with Mrs. Fighting Bear.

Friday went like Thursday but with one difference. Sarah was not to be seen. She didn't supervise the students at recess. She didn't even come down for lunch. Only an overheard comment by a student confirmed she was at the school.

As I finished the after-lunch mopping, Mrs. Fighting Bear barked, "Dump water. Then go. I don't need ya next week. Sarah hired me a helper, a really good helper."

I instantly realized that Sarah's demure glances, her affectionate pat on the shoulder, and her beguiling smile were tools taken from the bag of tricks women have been using since time immemorial to melt men's hearts, addle our minds, and get us to do their bidding. The sorceress had used those tools to achieve her purpose: Be Mrs. Fighting Bear's unpaid assistant while she searched for a Cheynne woman to do the job. Employment was hard to come by on the reservation, and some tribal member needed this job. I understood that. Yet, I was pissed, to put it mildly.

I dumped the dirty mop water down the drain sink, got into my pickup, and put the Birney Day School in my rearview mirror. Upon reaching my camp on Poker Jim Creek, I hastily struck my tent, threw everything into my pickup, and departed.

At the main road, there was a choice—head north or go south. Wanting to put distance between me and the Birney Day School quickly, I leaned over to get a map out of the glove box. As I did, an envelope on the dashboard caught my eye; it contained a note:

> *Take the Lame Deer Road for three miles.*
> *You will come to a trail coming in from the right.*
> *Follow it for a mile and a half. When you come*
> *to a rock outcropping on your right, stop. I will meet you*
> *there after school.*

The note wasn't signed, but it didn't need a name. A butterfly that hadn't been heard from since I struggled to find the courage to ask the most attractive girl in my senior class to the high school prom started flying around in my stomach.

CHAPTER FOUR

A Lesson from the Top of a Mountain

*"A change of perspective comes with climbing the mountain set
before you."*

Ten Fingers, Oglala Sioux

At fifteen minutes to four, puffs of dust rose from the trail I had just taken. Soon, a dented 1946 Ford that listed to the left like a sailboat running abeam a starboard wind appeared. The car drew within ten feet of me and stopped. Its door groaned open, and Sarah lithely slipped out. As she did, doubts sprang up in my mind and waved red flags. Maybe the woman who had captivated my thoughts all week was an illusion created by needy loneliness. Perhaps her charms would pale in the bright light of familiarity. Possibly, she was just another attractive woman upon whose delectable shoulders sat an empty cranium. However, as Sarah approached, I was visited by my old nemesis—self-doubt. Maybe once Sarah got to know me, she wouldn't like me.

"Follow me," Sarah said as she put a rucksack on her back and headed for a nearby gigantic rock with a vertical face. Reaching it, she angled to the right, passed along the edge of the limestone outcropping, and began climbing the rock-strewn, nearly treeless mountain. As she led the way, I studied her. Sarah did not have youthful, set-your-hormones-raging sensuality. Instead, she was columbine-pretty—that delicate, translucent mountain flower with exterior petals of light pink that deepen at their base to lavender and fold around a center of four lily-white petals. The columbine does not do the slightest thing to be noticed except to climb into the sunlight a few inches above and slightly apart from competing weeds and nondescript foliage. Hikers, in their haste to find glory on mountain peaks, pass by a columbine without noticing its quiet beauty. When they do, the columbine does not lament. If uprooted and put into a carefully manicured garden, the flower loses its luster. A columbine grows best in the wild.

Sarah was tall, at least five-eight. She was lean and sinewy, built not for strength but for endurance. Her skin was the color of chocolate milk. She looked out at the world through eyes that took in everything while revealing nothing. Silky, black hair cascaded down her shoulders and fell nearly to her hips. Speaking of hips, her hips weren't the narrow hips typical of Indian women of the Northern Plains. The curves that filled Sarah's jeans could have been in a Calvin Klein ad. A Caucasian influence was not surprising. Whereas the Indians of the Northern Plains were some of the last Native Americans to be visited by Whites, they have been in contact with Caucasians for three hundred years. In 1724, a party of French explorers visited the Arikara villages on the upper Missouri River along the present-day North Dakota-South Dakota border. A decade later, specifically in 1738, Pierre La Vèrendrye and his party of Frenchmen came upon a Mandan village at the confluence of the Heart and Missouri Rivers near the present-day town of Mandan, North Dakota. The Frenchmen spent a week with the Mandan before going farther southwest. After a futile search for a route to the Pacific Ocean, they returned to their trading post near present-day Winnipeg, Canada. After that, Whitemen were frequent visitors to the Mandan and Hidatsa villages. These tribes believed that one man's power could be transmitted to another man if they had sex with the same woman. So, husbands freely offered their wives to the strange men from the north who had sticks that made loud booms and killed things at a distance, knives made of iron that readily sliced away the meat from a buffalo's bones, and many other things that bespoke of their strong medicine. Like many native beliefs, the wife-offering had a practical side. It widened the gene pool in villages where as few as a hundred lodges of people lived together generation after generation.

When the Lewis and Clark Expedition beached their keelboat and two pirogues at the mouth of the Knife River in present-day North Dakota in the late fall of 1804, they found five Whitemen living with the Mandan. One of them had been living there for fifteen years. By the time the forty-two Whitemen and the big strapping Negro, York, departed upriver in the spring of 1805, ethnic diversity on the Northern Plains was in full bloom. Since then, eight generations have come and gone. I suspect that, way back, there was a Frenchman in Sarah's ancestry.

The mountain was too steep for a direct assault. So, we ascended via a series of switchbacks. As we climbed, the air became thinner, starving my blood of oxygen. But Sarah did not slow down. "It's pretty country," I commented between gasps for air, hoping that the observation would occasion a short stop to look around long enough to enjoy the view and, most importantly, give me time to suck more oxygen into my lungs.

"I love this country!" Sarah replied without breaking stride.

Long after I lost count of the switchbacks, we reached the top and looked down on the world from one of the highest peaks the Wolf Mountains. In every direction, the land fell below us. Looking north, our eyes ricocheted along the spine of the Wolf Mountains. To the east, we saw the Tongue River following its serpentine route toward the Yellowstone. Casting our gaze to the south, we looked at a seemingly endless array of pine-studded hills. While these vistas were alluring, they paled compared to the view to the west—the Bighorn Mountains. Rising from the plains like the bulwark of a medieval city, the Bighorns demanded our attention. Snow-capped Cloud Peak was radiant in the late afternoon sun and appeared to be so close we could reach out and touch it. Actually, it was forty miles away.

Sweeping her arm across the 360 degrees of the horizon and exuding a broad smile, Sarah said, "This is the land of the Tsistsistas, or, as Whitemen call us, the Northern Cheyenne. Anthropologists tell us the Cheyenne descended from a tribe known as the Algonquins who, long ago, lived between Hudson Bay and the Great Lakes. I don't know much about that time because our oral history goes back only to when The People lived along the lakes and rivers of northern Minnesota. East of us lived the Chippewa. North of us were the Cree and the Assiniboine; all were our enemies. They were the first to have contact with the fur traders working their way west across Canada, and they traded beaver pelts to the Whitemen for guns. Cheyenne arrows and lances were no match for guns, and we were driven south. For a short time, we lived along the Minnesota River. But soon, our enemies again drove us out. We fled west onto the prairie. Hunger stalked us. Around seventeen hundred, our wanderings brought us to what is now southeast North Dakota. We settled along a river that still bears our name, the Sheyenne, and we no longer lived on fish but on buffalo.

"You know, don't you, that when one is afoot, the prairie is like an ocean, vast and endless. The Cheyenne lived well when the buffalo came north in the summer, but sometimes the buffalo did not come. Perhaps they were a three-day walk to the west, a two-day walk to the east, or maybe only a one-day walk to the south. No one knew. On foot, it was difficult to find buffalo amidst a sea of grass. When buffalo could not be found and the winter was long and bitter, many died of hunger."

I listened intently as she continued. "Around 1770 our old enemy, the Chippewa, again found us. They attacked while the men were out on a hunt. Many women and children were killed. Some were taken captive. The Chippewa burned our village to the ground. The Cheyenne who escaped fled west across the prairie, which brought us to the Missouri River. There, we found the Mandan and the Arikara. They were friendly; so, we, too, built earth lodges and lived in a village near what is now Fort Yates, North Dakota. About this time, we acquired horses. The horse opened the prairie to us. We abandoned our earth lodges and our fields of corn, squash, and beans to follow the buffalo. We became nomads and lived in easily moved buffalo-hide tepees. In our wanderings, we came upon the Black Hills. Soon, our hunting territory ran from the Missouri River west to the Bighorn Mountains and from the Yellowstone River south to the Arkansas River, but we made a special claim on the Black Hills and the land west of it clear to the Bighorns. Here, along the Powder and Tongue Rivers, the winters are not fierce like they are just to the north. In spring, breezes carry the fragrance of sage and pine, not the buzz of mosquitoes one hears in the flat land east of the Missouri River. Even in the heat of summer, the rivers run cool and clear, not stagnant and diseased like the water of the land farther to the south. Here, the prairie is covered with grasses that cure in the fall to provide feed for our horses through the winter and until green grass comes again in the spring.

"We loved this land and never wanted to leave it. A council was held. The elders decided it was better for us to die bravely in the prime of our lives defending this land than to run away and die as old people in a place less beautiful. The council concluded that our young braves should become the best fighters on the Plains, and they did. The Northern Cheyenne fought ferocious wars against the Kiowa, the Pawnee, the Shoshone, and the Crow for this land. We gave our blood for it."

Pausing in her story, Sarah dug into her rucksack and retrieved two bottles of Coke. Handing me one, she continued.

"But in 1851 and again in 1868, the Cheyenne, Arapahoe, and Lakota signed treaties with the U.S. Government. The Fort Laramie Treaty of 1868 said the land west of the Black Hills to the Bighorns was unceded Indian Territory, which meant it belonged in common to all the tribes that signed the treaty. But in 1874, Custer violated the treaty by marching with a thousand soldiers into the Black Hills to find what he was looking for, gold. Whites soon crawled into the Black Hills by the thousands. They dug up Mother Earth to get yellow metal. When the government did not honor its promise to keep the gold seekers out, our allies, the Lakota, tried to defend their land. Their warriors killed many of the trespassers and put such a fright in others that they turned back. Yet, the greedy spiders continued to come. So, the U.S. Government decided it was better for its soldiers to fight Indians than to stop Whitemen from stealing our treaty-given land. But to make war on the Lakota and the Cheyenne, a pretext was needed; the government created one. In January of 1876, they sent out runners to tell the Indians living in the unceded Indian Territory that they had to come into an agency. If they did not, soldiers would come to hunt them. Our chiefs concluded that breaking camp and traveling hundreds of miles across the prairie in the dead of winter made no sense. Anyway, the government had no right to order us to move. This was our land. It was ours by heritage and by treaty. We stayed in our winter villages. That summer, the summer of 1876, the army came looking for us. Custer passed nearby. He thought he was coming to kill more Indians, but the promise-breaker was looking for a hill to die on.

"The Lakota and the Cheyenne were camped on the Little Bighorn River. The Cheyenne were the farthest downstream. Above them were the camps of the Oglala, the Miniconjou, the Brulé, and finally, the Hunkpapa—all bands of Lakota Sioux. Custer's scouts saw only the band of Sioux camped the farthest upstream, Sitting Bull's Hunkpapa band. Custer ordered a small group of his command to attack them from the south. As these soldiers charged the Hunkpapa village, they suddenly realized that nearly the entire Lakota Nation and many Cheyenne were camped along the river. The soldiers retreated, but it was too late. Most of them died there. While this was happening, Custer was trying to get in behind the Hunkpapa to cut off their escape. To do this, he descended a ridge leading toward the river. Seeing soldiers advancing toward them, the Cheyenne and Crazy Horse's band of Oglala crossed the river to fight them. That day, we got our revenge on Custer for massacring helpless Southern Cheyenne women and children camped along the Washita River in Oklahoma."

Sarah then fell quiet. Her eyes traveled to the western horizon and revisited her ancestors' glorious victory at the Little Bighorn. But when she again looked at me, her eyes brimmed with tears.

"Even while the battle was going on and victory was in the wind, the women were striking camp. They knew the army would want revenge. That fall, three thousand troops combed the Powder River country, hunting for Indians. We dispersed to the four directions. Two Moon led his band to Fort Keogh, where they surrendered to Colonel Miles. Dull Knife and Little Wolf took their bands to Fort Robinson and surrendered. Some Cheyenne went to live with the Arapaho on the Wind River Reservation in Wyoming. Wild Hog and Little Chief joined the Southern Cheyenne in Indian Territory, what is now Oklahoma.

"Years later, after many Cheyenne had died and there had been much suffering, we have slowly and gradually come back home. The first to come back were Two Moon's band. They returned in the spring of 1880 when Colonel Miles allowed them to return to their land along Rosebud Creek. In 1884, President Arthur designated 371,000 acres along Rosebud Creek as a home for the Northern Cheyenne. But there were problems. Many Whites had taken up homesteads in the area, leaving it a checkerboard of land owned by Whitemen amongst reservation land. And the reservation's boundaries were not well determined along the eastern side, resulting in the Whites claiming land the Cheyenne considered theirs. To make matters worse, there were too many Cheyenne and not enough rations. To ward off starvation, some Cheyenne took to killing Whitemen's cattle and sheep. A couple of foolish young Cheyenne men killed a sheepherder. There was so much tension on both sides that it seemed the white homesteaders and the Cheyenne might go to war. In 1898, the government sent a man named McLaughlin to straighten things out. He had been the Indian agent for the Standing Rock Reservation and had an Indian wife and mixed-blood children. He understood us and our plight. McLaughlin decided the reservation should be enlarged by extending its eastern border to the Tongue River, and all Whites living on the reservation should be bought out and made to leave. In 1900, President McKinley put McLaughlin's suggestions into an executive order. Today, we have our own reservation. It's only 460,000 acres; its not much, but it's ours. This time, we will stay!"

It was not clear whether we had climbed the mountain so that, from its vista, Sarah could tell me the history of her people, or if the story had come out in the spontaneity of the moment. For me, the events Sarah related were historical. For her, the tribe's history was personal and relating it caused her palpable emotional pain.

"Are you alright?" I asked.

A look of confusion flashed across her face. Then, smiling, she replied "Yes, I am alright. And haho'. Haho' for listening. I sometimes surprise myself by how much anger there still is in me." Standing, she said, "The sun will set soon, we must go."

The sun disappeared behind the Bighorn Mountains as we worked our way down, and the night was moonless. Everything was black. When I tripped over a protruding rock and nearly fell,

Sarah, seeming to possess the night vision of an owl, took my hand and led me down the mountain. Upon reaching our vehicles, she gave my hand an affectionate squeeze. I sensed she was waiting for a hug, that reassuring embrace two people share after experiencing something that touched them deeply. I held out my arms, expecting her to fold herself into them. Instead, Sarah walked to her car and slipped into the driver's seat. A starter groaned ominously as its teeth gnashed against the flywheel. None too soon, the engine screamed to life under a foot heavy on the gas pedal. Headlights came on, and the Ford swung in an arc. Poised to retrace its steps, the car stopped beside me. Rolling the window down, Sarah looked expectantly at me and asked, "Will I see you Monday?"

"Mrs. Fighting Bear told me that you hired a helper for her, and she doesn't need me. I interpreted that to mean you wanted me to go."

Sarah flashed a confused look. Seemingly uncertain of what to say, she pushed her tongue against her front teeth as if they might find an answer. For an agonizingly long half minute, no words came forth. Finally, she spoke. "Thursday, you said you'd work for Maggie one more day. I thought you wanted to leave."

"No." I mumbled. "I don't want to leave."

We each searched for words, any words that would give us a solution to our problem. It was Sarah who found them. "If I find work for you at the school, even if it's unpaid work, will you be there?"

"Yes! I'll be there."

"Epeva'e," she said softly and drove off into the night.

CHAPTER FIVE

Miles City, Montana

The road ahead can be treacherous,
and it sometimes leads to temptation.

Saturday morning brought a cold drizzle that filled the Tongue River Valley with fog. Only the tops of the hills poked up through the brew, and even they did not find sunlight. A thousand feet above them, dark clouds wept on their nearly bald heads. Realizing that Poker Jim Creek was going to be a gloomy place to spend the weekend, I heard civilization calling. In that remote corner of southeast Montana, civilization was any town big enough to have a stop light. Miles City was the only town within a hundred miles that qualified, barely. Originally called Milestown, it sprang up in 1876 in the form of two saloons and a gambling establishment adjacent to the newly established Fort Keogh under the command of Colonel Nelson Miles. When the Northern Pacific Railroad arrived in 1882, Milestown became known as Miles City, and it became a shipping point for ranchers marketing their cattle in Chicago. The wide-open town had forty-two saloons that sold one thousand bottles of beer a day and thirteen hundred gallons of whiskey a month.

Poker Jim Creek is connected to Miles City by a dirt road that winds down the Tongue River Valley. That morning, the road was rain-slick. If a curve was taken too fast, there was not enough traction in the gumbo to keep my pickup from going off the road's left shoulder. If a turn was taken too slowly, the pickup tried to slide down the grade and into the ditch. Being sandwiched between too much and too little speed, prudence prevailed. The distance to Miles

City was a lot farther than the map suggested.

At last, there was a speed-begging straight-away. I barreled down the road at an exhilarating forty miles an hour. Then it came, an unannounced ninety-degree turn. Because any attempt to make the turn invited a rollover, I took the water-filled ditch straight on. Luckily, the vehicle had enough momentum to enable it, with a bit of help from the accelerator, to splash through the water and sink its teeth into the sod on the far side of the ditch. With its rear wheels slinging mud, the 172-horse chariot slid sideways across the prairie until the front tires caught hold of a tuft of sagebrush and jerked the pickup into a skidding U-turn. After another bounce into and out of the ditch, I was again headed to Miles City, albeit slowly. The Tongue River Road was Montana's approach to population control.

It was well past noon when Miles City finally came into view. The first stop was the Ford Garage for brushes, bushings, points, condenser, and spark plugs for a 1946 Ford. Finding a place to wash clothes was next on the chore list. A dangling sign on a side street revealed that a laundromat was hiding between a run-down bar and a seedy hotel. There was not a customer in the place, and for good reason. The laundromat was dark, dingy, and dirty.

While my clothes were taking a spin in the washing machine, I looked around for something to occupy my time. There wasn't much: a year-old *Newsweek*, a six-month-old *Life*, a recent edition of *Good Housekeeping,* and a well-worn paperback by some guy called Louis L'Amour. The title was *Hondo.* WESTERN was branded across a corner of the cover as if the moniker was a calling card. Out of desperation, I picked it up and started reading. As I neared the end of Chapter One, the door opened, and a tall, lanky lad of about twenty-two walked in. He was clad in manure-coated cowboy boots, blue jeans, a red flannel shirt that had faded to pink, a threadbare Levi jacket, and a black cowboy hat that might have been big enough to hide half of Montana but could not conceal his shock of carrot-red hair. Everything about the cowboy said, "Ah shucks."

The cowboy dumped the contents of his duffle bag—white underwear, black socks, a white shirt, three pairs of blue jeans, and several red bandanas—into a washing machine and plugged it with a quarter. His name, CLAUDE, was etched into the backside of his leather belt. Putting a hefty pinch of chewing tobacco in his mouth, Claude sat down to wait. When he settled, I asked, "What brings you to town?"

"Clothes," Claude replied, looking puzzled that anyone could be so dumb as to ask for an explanation of the obvious. Taking a discerning look at me, Claude's expression of puzzlement changed to one of sympathy. "They're dirty," he explained. "Need washin'."

With a little prompt, Claude told me his story. He was born and raised on a ranch in Wyoming. For the last four years, ever since graduating from high school, he had worked for a big sheepman north of Miles City as a herder. The sheep had been his constant companion from May through August. Now, the lambs were being weaned, and the ewes were being culled, giving Claude a few days for himself. While my clothes were spinning in the dryer, Claude related the highlights of Miles City. One of the things he mentioned piqued my curiosity.

By the time my clothes were dry, the rain had taken a hiatus. I set out to investigate what Claude considered to be Miles City's most interesting attraction. Per his directions, I strode west down Main Street. From the Stockman Café to the Stock Growers Bank, the Miles City Saddlery, and the Montana Bar, Miles City had all the earmarks of a cattle town. It could have been Dodge City, Kansas in 1870, or, for that matter, Miles City, Montana, circa 1882. Just like those early-day cow-towns, the whorehouses were located at the west end of Main Street. That made sense. In the heyday of these frontier towns, conformity, propriety, and all those things that shackled a man and crimped his lifestyle arrived on a horse-drawn stage from the East. Intending to fight virtue mile by mile, block by block, or, if necessary, store by store, the proprietors of these houses of ill-repute located them as far from civilization as possible, the west edge of town.

The whorehouses in Miles City were two well-maintained, ranch-style houses. One was painted a dull yellow. The other was drab brown. It was unclear whether the two houses were in competition or if a booming business warranted expansion. The light-yellow house struck my fancy.

The waiting room was like any western bar. A wood counter ran the length of the west wall. Six booths were tucked against the north wall. To my right were a half-dozen small, round tables with wooden chairs. I sat at the table in the far corner. It was late afternoon. The only people in the place were three men playing cards. They did not look up or even turn an eye, yet I felt scrutinized. After five minutes, one of the card players got out of his chair and ambled toward me. He wore a rust-brown cowboy hat, a half-buttoned western shirt that tried in vain to hold in his beer belly, faded jeans, and cowboy boots. He stopped six feet away and glared at me, apparently waiting for me to say something. Nothing about the man's appearance gave me a clue as to what he wanted; so, I shrugged my shoulders.

"What do ya want?" he snarled.

"What do I want?"

"To drink," he asked with exasperation.

"A rum and coke will do."

The cowboy reduced to a bartender, or perhaps the bartender wannabe cowboy, went behind the bar and poured a drink. With it in hand, he strode back and plunked the glass down on the table, spilling some of it.

"How much?" I asked.

"I'll start a tab," the bartender said over his shoulder as he strolled back to his card game.

There was not a woman in sight. This wasn't looking like a whorehouse. At least, it did not have the appearance I imagined such an establishment would have. Could it be that at that very moment Claude was driving back to his sheep ranch and grinning ear to ear in anticipation of telling his sheep how he'd pulled one over on an eastern dude?

The rum and coke had to be drunk carefully because any sudden movement caused the ice cubes to clang against the side of the glass. In the silence of the place, the clink of an ice cube against glass sounded like the peal of a church bell. Not exactly the refrain one wanted to play in a whorehouse.

Eventually, two women emerged from a hallway. One was tall and slim; the other wasn't. While looking me over, they whispered to each other. Coming to an agreement, the tall one came over and sat in the chair beside me. "It's twenty for the regular," she announced, lewdly running her fingers along my thigh. I shook my embarrassed head from side to side. "Do you fancy Glenda?" she asked, bobbing her head toward her partner, who was leaning against the bar. Hearing her name, Glenda wormed out of her stupor. She slowly and suggestively slid her hand up her oversized, short thigh and batted her mascara-laden eyes at me.

"No, I don't think I do."

The tall woman stood up and walked away. Passing the bartender, she gave him an 'oh well, I tried' shrug of the shoulders.

For the next thirty minutes, no one came, no one left, and no one said anything. It was just the occasional sound of an ice cube inadvertently clinked against the side of a glass, the muted rumble of a deck of cards being shuffled, and the occasional tap of a heavy finger on the wooden table. The tap on the table was a code. It meant the player wanted another card. After that bit of clever detective work, there weren't any more whorehouse mysteries to be solved. It was time to go.

"How much?" I asked the bartender.

"Catch ya next time," he grunted without looking up.

In the morning, it was dull gray outside the motel window. Low-lying clouds had returned to spit rain in the face of anyone who ventured onto the street. Having seen all there was to see and having done all that there was to do in Miles City, it was time to leave. The Tongue River Road was still slick and treacherous, making it a slow trip back to Poker Jim Creek.

CHAPTER SIX

Finding My Calling

The truth always comes out.

When the sun peered into the Tongue River Valley Monday morning, it saw dark clouds slinking around like adolescent ruffians reluctant to clear the street after a night of owning the town. At school, it was time for recess, but the grass was too wet for the children to play outdoors. They stayed in their classrooms, presumably playing indoor games. In the lunchroom, my replacement, an Indian girl who looked to be about seventeen, was washing the lunchroom tables.

"Hi," I said congenially. "You must be Mrs. Fighting Bear's helper. My name is Jonathan." She looked down at her dishrag and didn't say anything. Not wanting our first interaction to end on a low note, I asked, "And your name is?"

"Dawn," she whispered, focusing her eyes on the lunchroom table.

Seeking redemption for making her uncomfortable, I lamely commented, "You'll enjoy working here, Dawn. It's a nice school." She scrubbed the table even harder. Realizing that no words would lessen Dawn's distress, I banished myself to the janitor's workroom.

Mr. Fighting Bear was standing with his back to the door, talking to himself. "You has got to be here somewhere," he muttered, running his fingers through a box of tools. "There ya be," he announced, enthusiastically holding a putty knife over his head. Then he went back to rummaging. "Okay, ya little bastard, I know there's another of ya in here somewhere. But where are ya?" A few seconds later, Joe came up with a second putty knife, which he again held up with trophy-like enthusiasm.

"Good morning, Mr. Fighting Bear," I said to announce my presence.

"Mornin'," he replied, turning to greet me with a grin on his face. "I hear ya is gonna help me putty windows. Do ya know how, or do I have to teach ya?"

"I'll do one pane, and you can inspect my work. How's that?" He nodded and led the way outside.

The schoolhouse had twenty-five windows, each with twelve panes, making a total of three hundred windowpanes. There were also eight casement windows, two at each corner of the foundation. We started on the two casement windows in the northeast corner. After we had worked for five minutes, Mr. Fighting Bear reached over and lightly tapped the back of his putty knife on the windowpane I had just finished caulking. "Humpf," he grunted and went back to working on his windowpane without further comment.

Laying out a line of putty, I said, "Were you born here along the Tongue River, Mr. Fighting Bear?"

"Call me Joe. And no, I'm not from here."

"Oh. What tribe are you?"

"I'm not Indian!" he replied curtly.

Joe Fighting Bear had black hair, brown eyes, light-brown skin, and a name that sounded like he was a Native American. But if Joe said that he wasn't Indian, so be it. In silence, we worked on our respective windows, finishing them at the same time. As we walked toward the casement windows at the southeast corner of the foundation, Joe looked around to ensure no one could overhear him and then quietly said, "I'm Métis." (pronounced *May'tis*)

"Métis?"

"Ya," Joe said, putting down his putty knife and propping himself against the foundation. Furrowing his brow as if doing deep soul-searching, Joe took out his sack of Bull Durham and cigarette papers. He carefully rolled a cigarette, lit it, and inhaled. After holding it in his lungs for a while, he slowly exhaled. The smoke floated upward and dissipated into the air. "A Métis is a mix of the French and the Indian," Joe explained. "It's a mix that goes back to the days of the voyageurs. Most voyageurs were Métis, eh? The Métis paddled freight canoes from one end of Canada the other. Some of them became middle-men traders, traveling to the far-flung Indian villages to barter trade goods for furs, and then bringin' the furs back to the post and swappin' 'em with the post factor for those things that make life easy. We didn't live in the trading' post, and we didn't live in the bush with the Indians either. We lived in villages that grew up near the tradin' posts, and the Métis became a group of their own."

"Joe, if the Métis are the product of Frenchmen marrying Indian women, then what is the difference between a Métis and a mixed-blood?"

Rolling his eyes, Joe took a drag on his cigarette that was so long and so deep it seemed he was sucking the answer out of the nicotine. Eventually, he exhaled. "A priest," he said, flashing a devilish grin and slapping himself on the leg in self-appreciation of his humor.

"A priest?"

"Ya, a priest. Ya see, the Métis stuck close to the French side of the family so they could live the good life—things like coffee and little metal spoons to stir in the sugar. We had metal pans, cast-iron cook stoves, shoes with hard soles, and linens for weddings. All those things that make for the good life. With the French came the priests. We Métis is Catholic, make no mistake about that! A Métis nearly always marries another Métis. So, the Métis became their own race with their own language, Michif."

Before going on, Joe took another pull on his cigarette. Exhaling, he continued, "A mixed blood is what happened when a tepee-crawling Frenchman had a quickie with an Indian woman. Not knowing she was in a family way, the Indian woman went with her tribe off into the bush. Surprise, surprise, along comes a baby. Now God likes the dark color over the light color nearly every chance he gets, so the kid looked Indian, and it sure enough was raised Indian. And that is what makes a mixed blood." With that, Joe snuffed out his cigarette, signaling he was done talking, and it was time we went back to work.

It wasn't long before my curiosity got to me again. "So, your name, Fighting Bear, is a Métis name. Is it common for the Métis to have Indian-sounding names?"

Joe did not respond, and the grimace on his face suggested the question offended him. We worked in silence for the next ten minutes. Just when it seemed that Joe had no intention of explaining his last name, he cleared his throat and, talking more to the window than to me, said, "Fightin' Bear is the wife's name. My name's LaFromboise. LaFromboise is a good Métis name on The Turtle Mountain Rez. When the Métis was drifting around, not White and not quite Indian, Little Shell, the chief of The Chippewa, took his Métis cousins into his tribe so he could claim more people and argue with the government for a bigger reservation. It was another joke the government played on the Indians. The government refused to count the Métis when it came time to fix how big a rez the Chippewa would get. That let the government take a lot of land the Chippewa thought was theirs. And to beat that, the government gives the Chippewa a mere ten cents an acre for some of the best farm ground in the world. To this day, the Chippewa call it the Ten Cent Treaty.

"I was born on The Turtle Mountain Rez, but we moved out of Belcourt and off the rez when I was twelve and went to Malta, Montana. I went to school with a mix of kids, some Chippewa, some Métis, and some White. We all pretty much got along." Looking at his watch, Joe said, "It's eatin' time."

We were finishing our meal when the students came rolling down the stairs, sweeping Sarah with them. As Sarah passed behind me, she gave me a pat on my shoulder before taking her place in the lunch line. Upon witnessing that, Joe abruptly stood up and went outside. Apparently, Sarah's gesture of affection had upset Joe. But what, if anything, could I do about it? With no clear plan for smoothing Joe's ruffled feathers, I went outside to find him.

He was sitting along the south side of the building, looking straight ahead with eyes that did not want to see me. As I sat beside Joe, he took a deep drag on his cigarette and held it in his lungs a long time before exhaling. As the smoke wafted upward, he said, "There are two types of white folk that come to the rez. I'm wondering which one of them you are."

"Two types?"

"Ya. There are those that grow their hair long and put it into a braid. They hang a dream catcher from the rearview mirror of their outfit and go to every powwow they can locate. They drive a Volkswagen van with flowers painted on it. They are wannabe Indians. But you aren't a wannabe Indian. I got you pegged for the other kind."

"The other kind?"

"Them that wants to save the Indians. We can tell 'em right off. Like you, they don't have dirt under their fingernails or callouses on their hands. Like you, they drive a brand new, shiny outfit. During their growing up years, they learned about the awful things the government did to the Indians, and that makes 'em feel guilty. So, they come out here to wash away their guilt by trying to save the Indians. Well, I'm tellin' ya right here and now, Mr. Wagner, the Cheyenne don't need you to save them. It would be best for us and best for you if ya got in your shiny new pickup and went back to where ya came from."

Several minutes of silence passed before I calmed myself enough to reply to Joe's baseless accusation.

"Joe, you are right. I am not a wannabe Indian. But I sure as hell did not come here to save the Cheyenne. The simple story is that I was more or less lost when I stumbled upon the Birney Day School.

"Lost? Lost is something that happens to fools and drunks. You ain't been lost since you were out of diapers."

"Maybe lost is not the right word. It would be more accurate to say that I was wandering. You see, in 1892 my grandfather went to western South Dakota to start ranching on the open range. Ranching went okay for four decades but then came the Dirty Thirties—six years of drought. When Roosevelt passed the Emergency Relief Act, the government paid ranchers eighteen dollars for a cow and seven dollars for a calf. My grandfather sold his skin-and-bones cows to Roosevelt. He eventually sold his entire ranch to the government for two dollars and sixty cents an acre, cleared his debts, and returned to North Carolina. But he missed his ranch, and he talked about it for the rest of his life. His stories kindled in me a desire to see the West.

"My widowed mother died a year ago, leaving a sizeable inheritance to my younger sister and me. I decided that rather than keep my nose to the grindstone, I would take time to savor being alive. So, I quit my job, bought a pickup, loaded it with camping gear, and headed west. But Ohio, Indiana, Illinois, and Iowa were mostly cornfields. They were the Midwest, not my grandfather's West. Another two hundred miles took me to Chamberlain, South Dakota, a small-town squatting on the east bank of the Missouri River. After crossing the river, the highway climbed a seven-mile-long hill that brought me to the top of the Missouri River Breaks where the seemingly endless prairie was fragrant with the smell of sage and the sweetness of wild clover. I felt like I was home.

"After driving another hundred miles, I was within sight of the White River Badlands, off to the south. It was tempting to go look them over, but I was on a mission and kept going. Twenty miles farther down the highway, a junction took me north a ways, and the next junction took me west to a little town called Cottonwood, my grandparents' hometown. I stopped at the town's one and only business, the Buckhorn Bar. The owner told me that there was only one person in town old enough to have known my grandparents. His name was Earl Eliason. I looked him up. Mr. Eliason did more than share stories and memories; he took me to my grandfather's ranch and introduced me to the present owners. In the spirit of Western hospitality, they showed me around the ranch and drew my attention to the things my grandfather had built that were still in use, including a corral made of logs he had cut and shaped with an axe. Touching them, I could feel his presence. But someone else now owned the ranch. There was no reason to linger. Besides, there was more of the West to see.

"The next evening, my pickup rattled across the plank-covered bridge over the Tongue River and brought me to the Birney Day School. The schoolhouse looked abandoned, and its grass looked like a good place to camp for the night. So, I did. In the morning, Sarah asked me if I'd help your wife. Then I met you and became a window caulker."

"That's some story, "Joe replied in a skeptical tone. "I'll chew on it. But for now, go get the ladder off the back of my pickup.

The windows on the north side are most in need of caulking. Start there."

Energy efficiency be damned, there were four big windows on the north side of the school, apparently provided so that during the winter months bored students could watch the snow squalls march up the river valley. Every pane on every window needed caulking. As I scrapped away the brittle caulk from the first pane, it gave way with a loud, protesting screech. A perturbed teacher came to the window. "That's too much noise," she said, tapping her finger against a glass pane to emphasize her directive. Her taps caused the windowpane to fall out and crash to the ground. "Oh my," she apologized, "I guess they need work. But do it quietly!"

At eleven fifteen, I went to the lunchroom to eat. Joe was nowhere to be seen. Mrs. Fighting Bear and Dawn were busy in the kitchen, but a tray of getting-cold food awaited me on a lunchroom table. I ate it and went back to work.

At one thirty, three elderly Indian women emerged from the tall sagebrush on the north side of the road and two others drove up in junkyard escapees—the five members of Mrs. Fighting Bear's coffee klatch. Each carried something into the school to be bartered for government commodities.

When school was about to let out for the day, and the last pane of the second window was being caulked, the crystalline silence was broken by a woman's voice. "Hey, Whiteman," the woman called out from the base of the ladder, "Whatcha doin' up thar?"

"Well, if youse has gotsta know," I said, doing my best to adopt a hillbilly drawl, "I'm a peepin' Tom. I has been up here on dis ladder all live-long day lookin' in dis here window, tryin' ta a get a glimpse of the purdy Indian woman that I heard tell haunts the place."

"And tell me," the woman drawled back at me, "whatcha gonna do wit' her when you find her?"

The deeper meaning of Sarah's question hit me square between the eyes, but before I could respond, I sneezed, and my nose started running.

"Come down here!" she commanded.

As my feet touched the ground, the school doors burst open and released an avalanche of students. Their energy set the earth spinning abnormally fast, and my legs went out from under me. "I must have caught the flu," I said, hanging onto the ground with both hands.

"Lucky if that's all you caught in Miles City!" Sarah said accusatively.

How did this woman know my every move? But right then, I didn't have the strength to compose the question or the energy to attend to the answer. My main objective was to keep from vomiting.

Sarah ran her fingers across the lymph nodes under my jaw. Reaching under my shirt, she felt the auxiliary nodes under my arms, took my pulse, and made me open my mouth and say 'ahh.'

"You're sick!" she announced. "You need something for it. Are you up for a short walk?"

"If it's short, and we walk slowly."

We walked south toward a bend in the river. As we approached the abandoned teachers' quarters, Sarah drew a folding knife from her jean pocket and severed the heads off several curly-top gum-weeds. After going a little farther, she used her knife to dig up the roots of several plants. She also collected the dried flowers of goldenrod, bark from a red-colored bush, and berries from wild prairie roses. But most of the plants she collected were unknown to me. At the river, Sarah scraped white fungus from the bark of a cottonwood tree. "I have what we need," she announced.

"What's that?" I asked, pointing a finger at the fungus. She only smiled.

Upon returning to the school, Sarah took her gatherings to the kitchen table and sorted through them. With my head throbbing and a fever-induced sweat popping out on my forehead, I collapsed into the chair beside Maggie's worktable. My leaded eyelids closed, and I perceived the world only by sound. A saucepan clinked as it was lifted from its hook, a faucet squeaked, and water gushed into a metal pan. A wood match was struck. The gas burner on the stove puffed to life. Sarah's footsteps went up the stairs. Soon, I heard her footsteps descend and enter the kitchen. Suddenly, the room was full of smoke! My eyes popped open. Looking around, I saw that the smoke was coming from a smudge Sarah was holding.

"Sweetgrass and juniper branches," she explained, waving the smoke over the plants, roots, and fungus she had collected. She slowly walked around me four times, fanning me with sweet-smelling smoke. Then, she used the smoking bundle like a broom and swept imaginary things off the kitchen floor, across the lunchroom, and out the basement door.

"What are you doing?" I asked.

"Getting rid of evil spirits. "You were covered with them! Obviously, you were someplace you shouldn't have been!"

Hearing the water boil, Sarah put the smudge into a tall glass jar. As the smoke wafted throughout the kitchen, she carefully scraped the pieces of bark, roots, flower heads, and fungus into her hand. Like a priestess dispersing sacrament, Sarah sprinkled her gleanings into the pot of boiling water and added one ingredient that made sense, brown sugar. Turning off the gas burner, she covered the pot and let the brew steep.

"And now what?" I asked with a discernably skeptical voice.

"Patience," she commanded, trying to make her eyes look stern.

As beads of sweat popped out on my forehead and covered my chest, Sarah rummaged through the cupboard for a coffee cup and a tea strainer. Finding them, she poured the hot brew through the strainer and into the cup. It sizzled upon encountering the cold porcelain. "Drink!" she said, thrusting the cup of hot, brownish-colored liquid toward my mouth.

"What is it?" I asked, putting a protective hand between my lips and the cup she was holding.

"It's medicine for your sickness," she answered, feigning impatience.

"Some plants are poisonous," I said with trepidation.

"Yes, and you should never forget that I know which ones. Now drink!"

"Where did you learn about this stuff?" I asked, continuing to resist her efforts to get me to drink the concoction.

"Stuff!" she scoffed. "I spent years learning about herbs and medicines from my grandmother, Nellie, and you call it stuff! Stop being a sissy. Drink!"

Hesitantly, I took a sip.

Wagging her finger at me like a doting but disappointed mother, she mockingly said, "You'll be a project." Putting her hand under the cup, she pushed it toward my mouth and made me drink every drop.

Tuesday dawned under a warm, obliging sky. Surprisingly, the fever and other flu symptoms were gone. It must have been a twenty-four-hour virus. I arrived at school at eight-thirty, feeling well enough to resume my caulking project.

At recess time, Joe came around the corner of the schoolhouse to where I was working and asked, "How's the caulkin' goin'?"

"Fine."

"Well, good workmen need good breaks. Let's take one."

We went to the south side of the building and leaned against the foundation to soak up the sun's warmth. Joe pulled on the string that perpetually dangled from the breast pocket of his faded jean jacket and out slithered his sack of Bull Durham. He rolled a cigarette, set it on fire, and took a long, contemplative drag. Warming to the sun and to each other, we watched Sarah play duck-duck-goose with the children. She found a private, personal way to let every child know he or she was special. She told Jessica Little Coyote that the barrette in her hair was beautiful, and a big smile planted itself on Jessica's face. Excitable Edgar Young Bird got so caught up in the game that he tagged the little girl he was chasing so hard she went crashing to the ground. A little later, Sarah was the fox. She tapped the girl beside Edgar and then raced around the circle, always just barely out of the pursuing girl's reach and dove into the empty spot. Pretending to be winded, Sarah leaned her head on Edgar's shoulder and whispered something in his ear. A sheepish grin flashed across his face. He took a deep breath, exhaled, and was again calm.

The children made sure that Sarah was often the fox. She chased one child after another. Even though she ran as effortlessly as the wind, any child who was overweight, slow, or clumsy always outran the fox. Joe and I watched as the sunlight glistened off the children's black, wind-tussled hair and put radiance in their cheeks. "They sure are having fun," he commented.

"Yes, they are."

While we watched the game of duck-duck-goose, Mrs. Johnson came to the basement door and stood there for a minute. If anyone saw Mrs. Johnson, they ignored her. When the teacher's patience was exhausted, which did not take long, she yelled, "Recess is over. Now get in here!"

Abruptly, the game ended. With heads down, eyes on the ground, and all traces of smiles wiped from their faces, the children obediently filed by Mrs. Johnson and went to their classrooms.

Joe didn't stir. He sat motionless and continued gazing at the empty playground. The look on his face suggested that, in his mind's eye, Sarah and the children were still playing duck–duck–goose. After several contemplative minutes, Joe said, "Ya have to make me one promise."

"What would that be?"

"You have to promise me that you'll take good care of her."

"I'll do my best."

"You damn well better!"

CHAPTER SEVEN

A Reluctant Reading Teacher

"Real knowledge is to know the extent of one's ignorance."

Confucius

Wednesday morning, the brittle caulk on the north-facing windows screamed for attention. It was gladly given as it felt good to be contributing to the school, and there was the added pleasure of working outside in the fresh air at a stress-free job. The life of a window-caulker was good.

At eleven o'clock, my serenity was interrupted by an irritated voice. "Come down here!" it demanded.

"What's the matter, Sarah?"

"We got a new student today, Lisa Spotted Elk. Her grandmother said Lisa was in the fourth grade in Hardin, so we put her in the fourth-grade classroom. Within an hour, the little girl was in tears. It seems that in her short life, the girl has been in and out of every school between Broadus and Billings, and she never stayed at any school for more than a couple of months. In the process, Lisa never learned to read. We've got to do something," Sarah concluded, looking at me expectantly.

"And?"

"And you'll teach her to read."

"Me? I don't know how to teach reading."

"You read, don't you?"

"Yes. But there's a big difference between knowing how to read and teaching someone else."

"You've already taught one person to read, yourself. Teaching the second person won't be hard. You'll work with Lisa for three, twenty-minute segments. The first one will be as soon as school starts in the morning, the second one will be after morning recess, and the third one will be after the noon recess. The first lesson begins today, after noon recess. You and Lisa can work in the lunchroom. It will be quiet in the lunchroom at that time." Without waiting for a reply, Sarah went back into the school.

When the noon recess was over and the children had returned to their classrooms, Sarah came down the stairs hand in hand with a waif whose unwashed hair hung down in a tangled web. The little girl wore a dress whose irregular hemline advertised it as a hand-me-down. The garment hung on her like a flour sack, hiding all of her except her skinny arms and legs. As Sarah and Lisa approached my "desk"—a lunchroom table—the ragamuffin peered out through her long hair. Seeing me, she froze. Sarah placed her hand in the middle of Lisa's back and gently pushed her forward.

When Lisa and Sarah were settled on the other side of the lunchroom table, I said, as cheerfully as an untrained, nervous reading teacher could muster, "Hi, Lisa. So, you've come for a reading lesson." Lisa's eyes stayed downcast. Her countenance could be summed up in one word, and that word was fear.

"You'll be fine," Sarah whispered into Lisa's ear. However, the tension in Lisa's body did not connote relaxation. Sarah shrugged as if to say, "It's your problem, deal with it," and she went upstairs.

As Lisa and I sat on our respective sides of the lunchroom table, each of us uncertain what to do next, I noticed Lisa didn't have a book with her. Fortunately, the school's small library was on four shelves in the back of the lunchroom. "Lisa, please help me find a book that looks interesting." Lisa didn't budge. So, I went to the bookshelf and selected a book with many pictures and few words. It was about dolphins. Returning to the table, I said, "Lisa, what do you know about dolphins?" After an awkward silence, I said, "Well, I know a lot about dolphins. Dolphins have four legs. They live in the Bighorn Mountains and eat grass. Right now, there are probably dolphins in the mountain meadows munching sweet clover."

"Dolphins don't live in the Bighorns," Lisa whispered.

"Oh, that's right. I must have confused dolphins with donkeys. So, where do dolphins live?" Lisa didn't answer.

Putting the book on the table so Lisa could look at the pictures, I began to read while running my finger under each word:

"Dolphins and porpoises are playful and intelligent relatives of whales. They have long inspired special feelings in people. Back in the days of sailing ships, dolphins often accompanied sailors on their journeys to distant and far lands, riding the waves created by the ship's bow cutting through the water. Ancient legends tell of dolphins making friends with people and even allowing them to ride on their backs."

If Lisa was listening, she didn't show it. At the end of the passage, I closed the book and said, "Reading is over for today, Lisa. I look forward to reading with you tomorrow morning." Even with my tacit permission to return to her classroom, Lisa didn't budge. "Lisa," I said, "You may return to your classroom." She lifted her twig-like legs over the bench and like a mouse creeping away from a rattlesnake, slowly slid one foot ahead of the other until she reached the bottom of the stairs. When her escape was assured, Lisa bound up the steps like a scared rabbit.

Within minutes, Sarah came down from her office. "How did the reading lesson go?"

"Reading is way down on the list of problems confronting that girl."

"What are her other problems?" Sarah asked guardedly.

"Well, there is the obvious chronic malnutrition and possibly another issue." Sarah raised her eyebrows to ask me to continue.

"Do you have any reason to think that Lisa might have been physically or even sexually abused?"

"What makes you say that?" Sarah asked defensively.

"Lisa didn't budge after you left. She sat there trembling in fear, scared to death. I think her fear had more to do with being alone with an adult male than it had to do with not being able to read."

Taking a deep breath, Sarah said, "It's possible. Maggie knows a bit about Lisa's background. Her life has not been good, even by reservation standards. For the past five years Lisa and her mother lived in abandoned cars and cheap rooms above bars. Who knows what happened during those years? Her mother died of cirrhosis last summer. Lisa is now living with her grandmother. But the past is the past. All we can do now is try to improve Lisa's life from here on."

"Maybe someone else should teach Lisa to read, someone who isn't a male."

"What would she learn from that? To continue all her life thinking that all adult males are to be feared. You'll teach her to read, and along the way you'll teach her that at least some of your gender can be kind and gentle and trusted."

Shortly after the start of school Thursday morning, Sarah and Lisa appeared at the bottom of the steps. "We're here for our reading lesson," Sarah cheerfully announced. Sarah might have been cheerful about the upcoming reading lesson, but Lisa wasn't. When Sarah prompted her to approach the lunchroom table, Lisa hid in the folds of Sarah's skirt. Again, Sarah put a hand on Lisa's back and gently but firmly prompted her to the lunchroom table. That being done, Sarah went back upstairs.

"Good morning, Lisa. Yesterday we read about dolphins. I forgot, but maybe you remember, where do dolphins live? Lisa looked down and didn't say a word. "Today, we will learn about Spotted Dolphins." I began reading from the book:

Spotted Dolphins can be up to seven feet long and weigh two hundred-eighty pounds. It is one of the fastest dolphins. They can swim twenty-five miles an hour. Their favorite food is Yellow Fin Tuna, but they also eat squid and small crabs.

The expression on Lisa's face suggested she wasn't hearing a word.

When the students went out for morning recess, Mrs. Fighting Bear intercepted Lisa and took her into the kitchen. There, she washed Lisa's hair, cut off the frayed ends, and braided it. By then, morning recess was over. The students came pouring through the lunchroom and went upstairs to their classrooms. When they were gone, Mrs. Fighting Bear put a bowl of ice cream covered with chocolate syrup in Lisa's hand and guided her to the lunchroom table. "I'll sit right beside you," Mrs. Fighting Bear said, patting the bench. "We will both learn about dolphins."

I immediately started to read:

"The sense of smell is absent in dolphins. However, they must have a sense of taste because individual dolphins have favorite foods. Because they are social animals, the sense of touch is important to them. They often touch each other, laying a flipper across another dolphin's back or swimming so close together their bodies brush, and they nose each other with their beaks."

Lisa put her head against Mrs. Fighting Bear's shoulder and peeked at the pictures.

When noon recess was over and the students came back into the school, Lisa was the last child through the door. Again, Mrs. Fighting Bear was waiting for her. This time, the cook put a bowl of bread pudding in Lisa's hands, guided her to the lunchroom table, and sat beside her. I read:

"Bottle-nosed Dolphins have excellent eyesight out of the water. It may seem strange that an aquatic animal should have such good eyesight in the air, but there are times, like when they feed on jumping fish, that their vision in the air is important."

As I read, Lisa's eyes trailed after my finger as it moved from word to word. We were making progress! That day, Lisa, Mrs. Fighting Bear, and I learned quite a few things about dolphins. More importantly, Lisa and I survived a shaky beginning. We could not have done it without the gruff cook's help.

CHAPTER EIGHT

An Allegory

It is amazing how much beauty a man fails to see until a woman gently draws him into her world and opens his eyes.

Monday ushered in another perfect fall day in southeastern Montana. Because there was only one ladder, caulking windows became a one-man job—mine. At fifteen minutes per windowpane, it would take seventy-five working hours to finish the task. I had job security!

While eating lunch, I asked Joe if it would be okay if I worked on Sarah's car that afternoon. "What's wrong with it? She drove it to school this morning."

"The starter needs new brushes. It also could use spark plugs and a general tune-up."

"Ya. I guess it does. Go do it, but we'll have to deduct that from your window caulking wages, eh?" he said with a broad grin.

After Lisa's final reading lesson of the day, I crawled under Sarah's car and found the starter hiding beneath an inch of grease and mud that had accumulated during a decade of neglect. Joe lay on his stomach, watching. As the last bolt came out and the starter was free, he said, "Hand it to me." Joe splashed gasoline over the starter and attacked it vigorously with a wire brush. When the crud had been removed, we opened the starter, replaced the bushings and brushes, and reinstalled it. We also replaced the spark plugs and installed new points and a condenser. While we worked on Sarah's car, Joe contentedly hummed a tune as he dipped his shoulders and waved his arms as if he were doing a jig.

When school got out, the teachers' voices, the children's laughter, the bang of Mrs. Fighting Bear's pots and pans, and all those things that breathe life into the school disappeared. I took the ladder down, laid it against the foundation, and went looking for Sarah. She was in the parking lot, standing beside her car with her rucksack in hand and laughter in her eyes. "Come," she said, gesturing toward her car. "There's a place I want to show you."

When she turned the ignition key, the old Ford burst out with life. "Somebody has been feeding my war pony oats," she said, feigning surprise. "Nea'esemeno."

"Nea'esemeno?"

"It means thank you."

"Joe helped."

"I'm lucky to have such good friends."

Sarah drove down the dirt road that led past the cemetery and paralleled the west side of the river. In three or so miles, we came to where tire tracks intersected the road. Turning left, Sarah eased her car off the road and onto the faint trail. The trail led us across a bone-dry hill sparsely covered with sagebrush. In less than a quarter of a mile, the tracks suddenly ended, and for good reason. We were at the top of a steep-sided ridge that ran east to west and overlooked a lush valley. Slipping and sliding down the steep hillside, we reached the valley floor. Surprisingly, at least to me, we came upon a beaver dam. On that windless afternoon, the water was a mirror. When the late afternoon sun cast our shadows on the pond, we simultaneously raised our arms to point at our shadows and laughed when the shadows pointed back at us. At the west end of the pond, a spring seeped out of the ground, making the earth soft and spongy and blurring the demarcation between prairie and pond. We started to circle around the back of the pond but found that the grass on the back side of the dam concealed soil so saturated with water that we sank to our ankles, forcing us to retreat and then increase the circumference of our circle around the pond.

The pond formed an ecosystem quite unlike the surrounding prairie. Near the water's edge, willows had taken root. Some of the bigger saplings appeared to have boldly marched into the pond. In truth, the beavers had progressively raised their dam until the water crept among the trees. As the water rose, the beavers had thinned the trees to add to their dam. Water lilies had arrived from only heaven-knew-where to take up residence in the pond's shallows. Farther up the draw, the willow saplings intermingled with cattails whose pods were poised to explode with life-giving seeds.

The water lilies, the willow trees, and the cattails were out of place in the rain shadow of the Bighorns. There was not another willow tree within several miles, a cattail within twenty, and only God knew how far it was to a water lily. The willow trees, the cattails, and the water lilies must have arrived as wind-born seeds. But the wind is capricious in the West, and it is seldom benevolent. Undoubtedly, the seeds were dropped in the same proportion on every square foot of prairie within fifty miles. Birds and small rodents likely ate most of the seeds, but a few surely fell into cracks in the parched earth. Finding protection, they lay dormant for months, maybe years, waiting patiently for the right moment—that perfect combination of temperature and rainfall. When it happened, the hard shell of the seeds softened and the inert life inside awakened. After ten days, a green sprout emerged. But by then, it was too late. The temperature was too hot and the moisture too little. The fragile green sprouts wilted and died. Yet, at this magical spot at the edge of the beaver dam, the seeds of the willow trees, cattails, and water lilies found the moisture they needed to sprout, the just-right temperature required to take root, and the conditions needed to thrive.

Gesturing toward the lushness, Sarah sighed, "Sometimes it seems that in this arid, barren, and bleak land everything is hopeless, nothing can flourish, and things can never get better. It takes a place like this to show us that beautiful, delicate things can grow here if only given a little nurturing."

"And to think that it all got started by a crazy beaver who found this place by dumb luck,"

"No!" Sarah countered, "This oasis was not created by a crazy beaver who had dumb luck. It was created by two lovers who had a dream and the courage to follow it. When the male beaver was little more than an adolescent, he fell in love with a young female beaver. However, the lady gave the impetuous young male no notice. He concluded that to get her attention he must prove himself to be a capable provider. So, he explored for miles up and down the Tongue

River for the best place to build a home. Finally, he found a clay bank that would allow him to dig a dry, warm den. The bank was beside a pool of water deep enough to not freeze to the bottom, even in the coldest winter. Nearby was a grove of aspen, good for honing beaver teeth. Not far upstream, there was a stand of succulent young cottonwood trees that would provide their winter larder. When the young male beaver discovered this wonderful place, he showed it to the lady of his desire.

"She was not impressed. But she saw that her suitor's intentions were good. Besides, his big, strong teeth were handsomely masculine, and his beady little eyes were cute. So, she showed her would-be lover where a rivulet of water trickled into the Tongue River. She pointed out that even though the water came off the parched prairie, the rivulet was cool, fresh, and clear. She told him that the rivulet continued to flow even on the hottest day of the driest month. She said that the source of the water had to be a spring, and she told him something more. She told him that if he accompanied her to the source of this rivulet, she would live with him and bear his children.

"He was uncertain of what to do. She was the most attractive beaver he had ever seen. Her coat was luxuriant. Her teeth were long and white. Her beady eyes twinkled. But he knew that crossing the prairie was fraught with danger and saw no reason to take a chance on the unknown when the familiar was safe, comforting, and sufficient. But in the end, he couldn't imagine life without her.

"The next evening, they set out just as the sun disappeared. Being beavers, they progressed slowly, very slowly, as they followed the rivulet all that night. When the sun came up in the morning, they were far out onto the prairie where, just as he had feared, they were vulnerable to predators. They hid as best they could in tall grass and waited anxiously while the sun slowly crawled across the sky. That evening, he wanted to return to the river's safety, but she would have none of it. 'Our future,' she told him, 'Is at the head of this trickle of water. If we want to find true happiness, we must have the courage to continue.'

"Reluctantly, he agreed to go on. That night, they again followed the trickle of water up the valley. But again, the sun found them.

They were even farther out on the barren prairie. Finally, at the end of the fourth night and just before sunrise, they came to the spring. They were tired, very tired. Nonetheless, they immediately started digging mud and collecting twigs to dam the little stream. They worked industriously every night to build the dam higher and stronger. In not much time, they were rewarded for their work. A pond formed behind the dam, and willow trees soon sprouted along its edges. The trees grew quickly, enabling the couple to add to their dam. As the pond grew, it backed up more water, resulting in more shoreline and a bigger area for trees to grow. The deep water of the enlarged pond protected them from their natural predators, and the location made them safe from their most feared predator, the trapper. No trapper would think of looking for beavers out in the dry river breaks. It was many years ago that the beavers first came to this spot. Now their children's children live here."

As we sat at the pond's edge sharing an apple Sarah had brought in her rucksack, I considered the many meanings of her allegory. There was the obvious: Women are smarter than men, and men, if they know what is good for them, will listen to women. There was also a subtle and certainly unintended meaning. It stemmed from Marshall McLuhan's observation that the medium is the message. Sarah's medium was perfectly spoken English punctuated with richly descriptive adjectives and metaphors. How was it, I wondered, that a child of the prairie, only two generations removed from her unschooled ancestors, could use beautiful prose to tell a cleverly crafted story? I wanted to ask her how she achieved her dexterity with the English language, but I had already learned that any attempt to learn more about the path that brought her to me only increased the distance between us. I would wait patiently for the answer to be revealed.

As we sat there admiring the beaver dam and the lush environment it had spawned, the sun slid towards the western horizon. But like the omnipotent warrior he is, the retreating sun mocked darkness by sending forth a rearguard action of vibrant pastel light that shimmered along a cloud bank stretched across the western horizon. "I SHALL RETURN," it prophesied.

As shadows descended, the Wolf Mountains sent down a cool

breeze. I unzipped my jacket and slipped it over Sarah's shoulder. She snuggled against me. Overhead, a sliver of moon showed itself. It was greeted by a chorus of yips, barks, yaps, and howls coming from farther up the valley.

"Coyotes!" I triumphally announced.

"One coyote," Sarah corrected. "Listen! He's talking about you. He has been watching you at your camp on Poker Jim Creek. He says that you can't sit still. You must always be doing something. He says you don't have the patience to wait for things to come to you. Instead, you walk around, scaring away the things you are looking for. He says you talk to yourself, even when no one is around to hear you. These things worry him. The coyote says we should be careful until we know more about this Ve'ho'e."

"What's a Ve'ho'e, a crazy person?"

"Well, almost. A Ve'ho'e is a Whiteman."

CHAPTER NINE

Chief Iron Head

Accidents occasionally lead to good outcomes.

When school dismissed Tuesday afternoon, Sarah was waiting for me beside her car. "Do you want to go back to the beaver dam?" I asked.

"No. It's pretty, but there are a hundred places I want to show you. Get in."

Sarah drove across the river bridge, went a couple of hundred yard, and parked her car. Opening the trunk, she retrieved a buck saw and a ball of twine. "Come," she said, walking toward some densely packed cottonwoods growing along the riverbank. The trees had grown tall and straight, but some of them had been choked off from sunlight and had died. Pointing at the tall, dead trees, Sarah said, "We will make a raft of them."

We cut down six, sawed them into ten-foot lengths, and carried the logs to the riverbank. We had a good start at lashing them together when darkness overtook us. "We'll finish tomorrow after school," Sarah assured me.

After school on Wednesday, we finished our raft. It was not a work of art, but it would float. "We will go rafting Saturday, and we will need two poles," Sarah said, pointing to a couple of dead saplings.

Saturday, we met in the school parking lot at noon and walked to where our yacht was waiting for us on the bank of the Tongue River. We nosed the craft into the river and were off. We had gone but a short distance when Sarah produced a couple of apples, a piece of cheese, and two bottles of Coke from her rucksack. As we ate, the river brought us a kaleidoscope of scenery. In a hundred crow-fly miles, the Tongue River merges with the Yellowstone, which meanders two hundred miles northeast to rendezvous with the Missouri. From there, it is only eighteen hundred miles to the confluence of the Big Muddy and the Mississippi River. I was a modern-day Huckleberry Finn, but I did not envy Huck his Jim. My rafting partner was much prettier.

The shadows lengthened in late afternoon, and beavers came out. While we were riding the slow-moving current, a beaver swam up beside the raft. When our human scent betrayed us, it smacked its tail, showering us in water, and dove. A little later, another beaver climbed aboard our raft and contentedly groomed itself while making little chomping sounds with its teeth. When it finished preening, the beaver slipped into the water and swam off.

As the sun set, we poled our way to the east bank and jumped off, leaving our yacht to continue to St. Louis without us. We climbed the riverbank and walked southeast, coming out on a grass landing strip for someone's small airplane. When we reached the end of the landing strip, a crescent moon appeared. It cast enough light to allow us to make out well-worn tire-tracks running south, parallel to the river. We followed them for three miles and came to the Tongue River Road, not far from where we had started. As a crow flies, we had not gone far.

When we got back to the school, Sarah put her arm around my waist and put her head on my shoulder. Intertwining her hand with mine, she pressed something into my palm. "It's a key to the school," she said. "There's a shower in the girls' bathroom. You should use it."

Monday, school marched at its usual pace. During noon recess, Joe and I took our reserved positions along the school's foundation to watch the children enjoy themselves. Sarah was playing hide and seek with the younger kids. The older boys were playing softball. Richard Kills-The-Crow was at bat. The pitch was perfect, perfect for a hitter like Richard. He hammered the ball. Out in shallow right field, Levi Jumping Elk saw that the ball was going to sail over his head, and he started for deep right field on a dead run while looking back at the flight of the softball.

"Watch out, Levi!" someone suddenly shouted. Levi turned to see what he should watch out for, but he kept running. With a thud, his head collided against the swing's horizontal brace bar. Ninety pounds of dead weight hit the ground with a thud. Blood gushed from his forehead and oozed from his mouth.

"Oh my God," Sarah whimpered as we knelt over the seemingly lifeless child. "Is he dead?"

Putting my finger on Levi's carotid, I searched for his pulse; it was weak and rapid, but it was a pulse. "He's not dead, but he's badly hurt. Sarah, is there a blanket in the school?"

"Yes. In the closet of my office."

"Get it."

I was still feeling Levi's neck and gingerly moving his head to determine whether any C1 to C7 vertebrae were broken when Sarah returned with a slate-gray army blanket. I laid the blanket beside Levi. "Joe, get over here beside me. Sarah, when we lift Levi, reach under him, grab the edge of the blanket, and pull it toward you so that when we put Levi down, it will be under him."

That was quickly done. Joe and Maggie got on one side of the blanket, and Sarah and I got on the other. We lifted Levi, carried him into the school, and laid him on a lunchroom table.

"Mrs. Fighting Bear, bring me a couple of clean washcloths and ice in a clean mixing bowl. Sarah, there's a brown leather bag in the far-back of my pickup. Please get it."

While Sarah was retrieving the leather bag, I scraped the dirt from under my fingernails and went to the bathroom to wash my hands thoroughly, using a generous amount of soap. When I returned to the lunchroom, Joe was standing beside Levi with one hand on the boy's chest to ensure he did not roll off the table. Maggie emerged from the kitchen carrying two clean washcloths and a bowl of ice. Sarah came rushing in with the leather bag. It contained what was needed—a syringe, Novocain, silk thread, and stitching needles of different shapes and sizes. I carefully pulled Levi's lacerated skin back to look at his skull. There weren't any bone chips or a fracture line. The blood pursing on his lips proved to be merely from a tooth-punctured tongue. While I was examining Levi, he slowly and with much effort opened his eyes. "What happened?" he groggily pleaded.

"You put a big dent in the swing, Levi. Can you move your toes on your right foot for me? Excellent. Move your toes on your left foot. Very good. Wiggle your fingers on your right hand. Now, wiggle your fingers of your left hand. Everything looks good, Levi. You're going to be all right. Now, lie still and close your eyes.

"Sarah, put ice in a washcloth and lay it on Levi's forehead about an inch above the laceration." While the ice-cooled washcloth was slowing the bleeding, I broke the syringe and a small needle out of their plastic protectors and filled the syringe with Novocain.

"Levi, I'm going to push a needle into the skin on your forehead. It will hurt a little. Are you up for that?" He nodded. As the needle was inserted, Levi didn't utter a sound.

"Are you a doctor?" Sarah asked incredulously.

"Once, before I became a window caulker."

"Thank God," Joe said.

After waiting five minutes for the Novocain to take effect, I lightly pressed the stitching needle against the skin just above Levi's cut. "Did you feel anything sharp pushing on your forehead, Levi?"

"Nope."

"Keep your eyes closed, and we will get you all fixed up." I pushed the stitching needle into his skin. He didn't flinch. The Novocain had worked its magic. The gash was closed with sixteen stitches. From somewhere, Sarah found a cot. We laid Levi on it. I checked his pulse, examined his pupil reflexes, pressed on his eyes to feel for resistance, and drew a pencil across his palm while watching for a twitch in his face. All the checks indicated he did not have hematoma.

Levi rested for the remainder of the day, but every hour I roused him to re-check for any indication that ruptured capillaries were spewing blood onto his brain. Between checks, I passed the time by reading articles in the *Readers Digest* found in the school's small library. At one thirty, Carol Standing Crow, a bright-eyed first-grade girl, came down the stairs. "How's Levi?" she asked, staring with apprehension at the stitches and the line of recently coagulated blood on Levi's swollen forehead.

"Levi's resting, and he's doing fine."

Carol looked closely at Levi to assure herself that my assessment was correct. Seeing Levi's chest rise and fall, she smiled. Looking at me, she asked, "Are you reading a doctor book about how to make him better?"

"Yes. It tells me how to help him. And Levi is going to be fine. His head is made of iron."

Carol's eyes grew big. Approaching Levi for a second look, she leaned over and looked intently at his head. "Iron?" she asked.

"Iron," I confirmed.

At two o'clock, Otto Washington, a third-grade boy, came down the stairs. "How's Chief Iron Head?" he whispered.

"Chief Iron Head is sleeping right now, but he's fine."

At two-thirty, Jasper Red Hat came down the stairs for the latest update. "How's Levi?" Jasper asked,

Levi was awake but resting with his eyes closed, and he answered for himself, "I'm okay. It's the swing that's broke."

In preparation for sending Levi home, I put a large, loose-fitting bandage over Levi's stitches and taped the bandage down at the edges to keep out dirt. When the school day ended, all the teachers and students tiptoed past Levi's cot to look at him and assure themselves he was on the road to recovery. When the teachers and students were gone, Joe, Maggie, and Sarah came over to where Levi lay on his cot. "Really, how is he?" Sarah whispered.

"He's as good as can be expected, but there is reason to be watchful."

"Watchful? Watchful for what?"

"I don't see any signs of intracranial bleeding, but it's too early to rule that out. I've written down the things his parents should look for. When you take Levi home, go over this note with them. If they see any of the things I've listed, they must immediately take Levi to the emergency room of the nearest, well-equipped hospital."

"You don't know what you're asking!" Sarah petulantly replied. "If there are concerns about Levi, you'll stay with him tonight!"

"Me?"

"Yes, you!"

"Where?"

"Here."

"Won't his parents be worried?"

"Levi lives with his grandmother in a two-room log cabin just beyond the tall sagebrush," Sarah said, gesturing to the north. "He looks after his grandmother as much as she looks after him. They don't have electricity, running water, phone, or a car. Joe and Maggie will stop by Mrs. Jumping Elk's place and tell her what happened to Levi and assure her that a doctor did a good job stitching the cut. They will tell Mrs. Jumping Elk that Levi will stay at the school for the night so the doctor can check on him." Noting my stunned look, Sarah added, "I'll stay, too."

As Joe and Maggie departed on their errand, Sarah walked over to Levi's cot and gently touched his hand. He didn't stir. Satisfied that Levi was resting comfortably, she disappeared upstairs. It sounded as if she was sliding furniture around. After fifteen minutes, she came down. "I'll get us something to eat," she said, disappearing into the kitchen.

Twenty minutes later, Sarah checked on the food she was warming in the oven. The oven door opened with a loud creak, and it woke Levi. "Where's everybody," he asked.

"Your classmates have gone home for the day. Sarah is in the kitchen, getting us something to eat. You are going to stay here tonight so Sarah and I can check on you."

The three of us were soon eating Maggie's leftover meatloaf, mashed potatoes, and string beans. Sarah even found some chocolate pudding for dessert. Levi merely picked at his food. Before long, he asked, "Can I go back to bed? I'm tired." He was sound asleep within minutes.

"Can you wash the dishes?" Sarah asked. Without waiting for an answer or announcing her intentions, she put on her jean jacket and slipped out the door. She was still gone when the sun went down, casting the valley in darkness. Inside the school, there were only two sounds: Levi's rhythmic breathing and the sound of the clock in the kitchen ticking off the seconds. Hardly noticeable at first, the ticks got progressively louder until they reverberated from wall to wall like rifle shots.

More than two hours passed before the basement door opened,

and Sarah stepped in from the night. She was carrying a laundry sack stuffed full of something. "Is he still asleep?" she asked.

"Yes, he is. Where were you?"

Ignoring the question, Sarah disappeared upstairs but soon came back. "Come," Sarah said, beckoning me to follow her up the stairs.

Previously, the upstairs had been off-limits for me. The forbidden territory begged to be explored, but it was dark, and Sarah did not turn on any lights. Nonetheless, I could discern certain features. At the top of the stairs, one could turn either right or left. There were four classrooms, two on the west side of the building and two on the east. An office was wedged between the two east-facing classrooms. Sarah disappeared into it. Following her, I smacked my knee into an unyielding object. "Sarah!" I called out, more than a little irritated.

"Stand still. Wait for your eyes to adapt." Gradually, forms and shapes appeared. I made out a desk, the one I smacked my knee into, emerged out of the darkness, a filing cabinet, and several chairs that had been slid against the north wall. After I had stood without moving for a few minutes, Sarah asked, "Can you see now?"

"A little."

"Good."

At that moment, a full moon rose in the east and peeked through the window. The moonlight revealed that Sarah was starting to undress. Wanting to look at her but not wanting to be caught doing it, I turned my head away from her only to find that the moonlight cast her shadow on the west wall. My eyes became glued to the silhouette as it reached down to her waist, grasped the bottom of her sweater, and pulled it up and over her head. My eyes remained fixated on the silhouette as her hands unsnapped her jeans and her hips undulated from side to side, inviting gravity to pull her jeans to the floor. The silhouette then slid down the wall and disappeared. After a long moment, I whispered, "Sarah?"

"Yes?"

"Where are you?"

"Down here."

"Oh," I said, standing motionless.

"Are you going to stand there all night, or are you going to lie down beside me?"

Inching my foot forward, I detected a thin mat covered with sheets and a blanket. Lying on it, I stretched myself thin along the edge, trying to take up as little space as possible.

"Silly Whiteman," she whispered.

"Yes?"

"It has to happen sometime," she said, unbuttoning my shirt.

Hesitantly, my fingers delineated the contours of her face, touched her forehead, felt her high cheekbones, traced the outline of her lips, and continued downward to the gentle contour of her shoulders. Emboldened, I explored the roundness of her breasts, the tautness of her stomach, and the smoothness of her thighs. That night, our bodies intertwined two souls and took a long time doing it.

CHAPTER TEN

The Medicine Wheel

*"As you walk upon the Sacred Earth,
treat each step as a prayer."*

Black Elk, Oglala Sioux

Darkness was no longer able to fend off dawn when Sarah shook my shoulder. "What would you like for breakfast?" she asked.

"Coffee and toast would be fine."

"You get all that stamina from coffee and toast? Amazing."

Upon reaching the bottom of the stairs, I immediately checked on Levi. Luck was with us. His pulse was steady, and his breathing was normal. There was no reason to wake him up. Besides, coffee and toast were waiting. Plum butter, the product of Maggie's bartering with the local women, added a touch of sweetness to the breakfast. Feeling cheerful, I looked at Sarah to see what was dancing in her eyes. But her eyes weren't dancing. They were perplexed and distant.

"What's wrong?"

"Nothing," she mumbled, staring into her coffee.

"From this side of the table, it doesn't look like nothing."

"I was thinking of the places I told you about when we hiked to the top of the mountain."

"What about them?"

"Did you like them?"

That was an odd question. Sarah had told me about the Northern Cheyenne's history. What was there to like or not like? But sensing there was more to her question, I selected the safest answer. "Yes."

"Me, too," she said, slowly stirring her coffee.

"What did you like about those places?"

"That is what is bothering me. I visited a few of the places when I was very young. Now, I hardly remember them. Most of them, I've only heard about."

"Would you like to see them?"

"Very much,"

"Can I have something to eat?" Levi interrupted, waking from his sleep.

"What would you like to eat, Levi?" Sarah asked.

"Whatever you're having."

Sarah fried him two eggs and served them with toast. While Levi ate his breakfast, he kept his eyes locked on the basement door. It was not long until the school's two vans simultaneously arrived. The students, led by Jasper Red Hat, came flooding into the lunchroom. Ceremoniously handing Levi a turkey feather, Jasper said, "You've earned the honor to wear this feather, Iron Head. My father says you are the first of our tribe to count coup on a swing."

As school was letting out for the day, Sarah came to the north side of the building where I was working. "Come to inspect my caulking?"

"No. That's Joe's job. I came to ask if Levi can go home tonight."

"Sure. He's doing fine. But he should keep his bandage on for a few days to keep out the dirt. Tell him not to wash his face any higher than the bottom of his nose. That way, no dirty water will seep into the sutures. If he can do that, things will be fine. We will change the bandage when he comes to school tomorrow."

"Good," Sarah replied. But instead of leaving to convey the okay to Levi, she stood there.

"Yes?" I asked, sensing there was more.

"If I had a place I might want to see, would you take me there sometime?"

"Sure."

"Good. Tomorrow bring your bedroll tomorrow and the things you will need for one or two days."

Tomorrow is Wednesday, Don't you mean Friday?"

"No. Tomorrow. The elders have approved it.

"Where will we be going?"

"It's a ways away and sort of hard to tell you. You'll just have to wait and see."

"Okay, I will wait and see, but what do you have in mind for us to do this evening?"

"Nothing. This evening, I meet with an elder and join him in a sweat."

"Who is this elder, and what do you mean 'join him in a sweat?'"

"Do I detect a bit of jealousy in your voice?" she said, not quite able to hide her satisfaction at the thought of me being jealous. "Not to worry, he's an old man, a medicine man. The sweat will purify my thoughts. When my mind is ready to learn, the medicine man will instruct me."

When school got out Wednesday, Sarah was late for our scheduled departure because a discipline problem with a student necessitated a discussion with the boy's parents. When the conference ended at 4:30, Sarah came out of the school and walked to her car. She retrieved a bedroll, her rucksack, a stuffed-full laundry bag, and a brown paper bag, and put them in the back of my pickup. Jauntily getting into the cab, she said. "Let's go."

"What direction?"

"East"

East immediately brought us to the Tongue River bridge and to a choice—north or south. Sarah gestured to the south. In five miles, we came upon a cluster of small houses nestled close to the road. It was Birney, or as the Indians call it, White Birney, a tiny village just off the southeast edge of the reservation. In the blink of an eye, we passed through White Birney, crossed over Hanging Woman Creek, and continued slowly up the rutted Tongue River Road. Sarah looked out the window with faraway eyes that suggested she was lost in thought. Wherever we were going, it was a long way away.

It was nearly six o'clock when we slipped by Decker, nothing more than a post office/general store. After another fourteen miles we reached pavement—Highway 87. To our left, the lights of Sheridan illuminated the horizon. I started to turn toward them, but Sarah instructed, "Go north." Eight miles bought us to the little town of Ranchester, where a Standard Oil gas station squatted on west side of the highway. Being low on gas, I pulled in. As I did, the station's lights went dark, and someone put a CLOSED sign in the window. But as my pickup rolled to a stop beside a gas pump, the station's lights came on, and a man stepped out the door. "It's lucky for you," the man said as he approached the pickup, "that I took one last look around before locking the door. You wouldn't find another filling station open for seventy miles."

The gas station was located at a junction. We turned left onto Highway 14 and in thirteen miles came to the base of a mountain whose side was so sheer that it seemed impossible for the highway to scale it. But that is what the highway did, twisting back on itself again and again while tenaciously clinging to the side of the mountain. After negotiating a seemingly endless series of switchbacks, we reached Bighorn's broad, flat top.

"Hungry?" Sarah asked.

"I thought you'd never ask!"

"Pull over, and we'll eat."

I pulled into the next accommodating meadow and stopped. Sarah retrieved her brown paper sack from the back of the pickup and pulled out two cooked potatoes, the legs and wings of a grouse, and two bottles of Coke. Sitting on the pickup's tailgate, we ate our supper. Overhead, stars stretched across the horizon from south to north like a giant neon sign that read I AM MAJESTIC! The fine print mocked, "And in the grand scheme of things, you are downright insignificant."

"That's E-kut-si-him-mi-yo," Sarah said, pointing to the Milky Way. "The spirit of one who has died follows the hanging road of the night to Heammawihio, the Creator. The deceased person's spirit joins Heammawihio in Seyan, which is what you call heaven. In Seyan, the dead live as they lived on earth in the old times. They hunt buffalo, steal horses from the Crow, and live in lodges made of buffalo hides."

"Where do the bad ones go?"

"Bad ones? The Cheyenne don't believe in hell, and we don't have a word for sin. What Whites call sin, we think of as simple mistakes or lapses in judgment, which all people make from time to time. When the Cheyenne die, all go to Seyan. Well, all but those who committed suicide or were extremely wicked."

In the southern sky, a sliver of the waxing moon seemed to be balanced on the spire of Cloud Peak. It conspired with the stars to bathe the Bighorns in a soft, yellow glow. But all too soon, it was time to continue our journey, wherever it was we were going.

In thirteen miles, we reached a fork in the highway, Sarah gestured toward the road on the right. Twenty miles further, she pointed to a meadow on the right-hand side of the highway and said, "Pull off."

The meadow was no different from the scores we had passed. But Sarah was definite. This was where she wanted to stop.

"Get your bedroll," Sarah directed as she put her rucksack on her back, her bedroll under one arm, and grabbed her stuffed-full laundry bag with the other. Carrying everything we needed for an overnight stay, which wasn't much, we traipsed northwest into a meadow so large the night swallowed it. After walking a a half mile, Sarah put a hand on my chest, bringing me to a halt. She walked ten yards to the east and stopped. Reaching into her rucksack, she produced a small object that, in the dark, I could not identify. She sat it on the ground, bowed her head, and offered what seemed to be a short prayer, spoken in Cheyenne. Walking back, she gestured for me to resume following her. Three quarters of mile brought us to the north edge of the meadow and the beginning of a canyon that cut a deep fissure into the side of the Bighorns. Fifteen or more miles away and far below us, pin-sized lights from ranch houses pierced the night. Sarah motioned for me to pause while she walked a short distance to the north and repeated the same ceremony-like actions she had performed at the previous stop. Angling west, Sarah found an animal trail and followed it. Where the trail started down into a deep canyon, she abandoned it. After making another offering, she continued westward. The moon had set, and darkness was everywhere, forcing us to feel our way across that rock-strewn terrain. After we had walked what must have been at least three miles, Sarah announced "We'll sleep here."

The ground was covered with small, jagged rocks. Nothing was level. It was a terrible place to camp. Nonetheless, I rolled out my bedroll. While I did, Sarah walked a short distance farther west, stacked three rocks on top of each other, and placed something on the top of the top rock. Coming back, she said, "We've been welcomed." She might have said more than that, but if she did I did not hear it because I instantly fell asleep.

Dawn was well advanced when I awoke and looked about. We were above timberline. Only a few shrubs grew at that altitude. They were scrawny, bent, and beaten up by the wind that relentlessly prowled the roof of the world. Twenty yards away was a large circle of made of limestone rocks. There were six, widely spaced, horseshoe-shaped clusters of rocks on the edge of the circle, each cluster being about eighteen inches high. The entire circle sloped gently to the west. Several miles to the east, a ridgeline blocked the morning sun from view, but its rays streamed overhead, lighting the sky above us to the brightness of midday while leaving the stone circle and the six clusters of rocks in shadow.

Sarah was standing in the middle of the circle, wearing a long skirt of red, black, and yellow calico cut into trapezoid-shaped patches arranged so the colors fanned out at the bottom of the skirt. The skirt was ornamented with flattened porcupine quills, small seashells, and elk teeth. She wore a long-sleeved muslin blouse and a knitted, light-gray shawl. Around her neck was a bear-claw necklace. On her feet were moccasins and beaded leggings disappeared under her skirt. She held a long-stemmed catlinite pipe in the crook of her arm. Lighting the pipe, she held the stem up to the heavens as if offering some spirit a smoke. She then pointed the stem down toward the earth. In like manner, she held the pipe out to the east, south, west, and north. After taking four puffs from the pipe, she raised her arms toward the heavens and spoke, presumably to a spirit. It was a short, fervent talk, softly spoken in Cheyenne.

Suddenly, the sun tipped the eastern ridge, and the fiery globe bathed the circle of rocks in the intense light of full day. A cluster of rocks on the east side of the circle was exactly between Sarah and the sun. When the sun's rays hit the cluster of rocks, it briefly shot out a clean, crisp shadow in the shape of an arrowhead. The arrow's pointed tip ended at Sarah's feet. She said a few more words, too softly for me to hear, reached into the pocket of her skirt for a small tin box, and tapped the ashes from the pipe into it. Then, she stepped out of the circle of rocks. Picking up her laundry bag and rucksack, Sarah walked north and disappeared over the canyon's edge. Apparently, nature was calling.

Leaving the warmth of my bedroll, I quickly dressed and walked over to the circle of rocks. The circle proved to be eighty feet in diameter. In the center of the circle, where Sarah had been standing, there was a circle of rocks approximately ten feet in diameter. Twenty-eight lines of rocks radiated from the center of the circle like spokes on a wheel to the outer rim. The medicine wheel was comprised of plate-sized white limestone rocks, and there was an abundance of them in every direction. The stones comprising the medicine wheel were half buried in dirt, suggesting they had been there for hundreds, perhaps a thousand years and well before the Arapaho, Crow and the Cheyenne arrived in the area.

While this celestial chronometer did not require remarkable strength to build, it required uncommon persistence. But in a timeless land, what was time? In one sense, time was so plentiful that might have seen meaningless to the indigenous people. In another sense, time brought about the significant changes in the Cheyennes' world. Before the coming of Whitemen, the Cheyennes' nomadic wandering across their vast territory was done in accordance with time. Their main measure of time was the sequence of full moons. During the moon of Enano'eese'he (June—the planting moon), the Cheyenne planted corn and squash along the rivers and creeks. In the moon of Meaneese'he (July), the Cheyenne gathered herbs in the Black Hills. They moved from place to place in accordance with the full moons.

Over the centuries the weather had taken its toll on each of the six rock clusters. During the winters, each cluster of rocks blocked the ceaselessly drifting snow, creating snowbanks up to and often exceeding ten feet. When spring arrived, the snow got wet, heavy, and slippery. In cahoots with gravity, the melting snow moved some of the stones in each cluster an appreciable distance downhill.

The cluster to the northwest was the one most in need of repair. It was essential that the cluster be restored as close as possible to its original form. Each dislodged stone had to go back into the same place the original builder had fitted it. Starting with the most recent insult to the cluster, I set out to find the missing stone. By looking at telltale lines left by encroaching lichen and using my finger to feel the little ridge of finely blown dust that marked the edge of the missing stone, I found it. I then searched for the next missing stone. In this manner, I carefully placed the dislodged stones exactly where the master builder had fitted it. Swelling with the pride of accomplishment, I worked diligently at putting the dislodged stones back to their original location.

Suddenly, a blood-curdling screech shattered the stillness. Looking up, I saw Sarah running toward me and waving her arms frantically. "Put that stone down!" she yelled, "You're a Ve'ho'e. You can't touch those stones!"

"I was just restoring the stones to their original place."

"Those stones are sacred," she angerly replied. "Even I couldn't put a stone back without the elders' permission. They'd never allow a Ve'ho'e to touch one!"

"Should I undo them?"

"No. You've already touched them once. To touch them yet again would only further anger Maiyum. The best thing we can do is to hope that no bad things happen to us because of this!" Taking my hand, Sarah led me away from the scene of my crime.

We hiked across an extension of the plateau that hooked to the northwest like a giant thumb and to where an animal trail led down the side of the mountain. Wanting water, we followed the trail into a canyon and came to a stream of clear, cold water skipping lightly over rocks. It quenched our thirst. We lingered there for several hours, appreciating the shade provided by towering ponderosa pine.

The hike back up was steep. It shortened even Sarah's long stride. When we finally reached the top, we sat on a rock ledge and rested our rubbery legs. As we enjoyed the panoramic view to the west, Sarah pulled venison jerky and two bottles of Coke out of her rucksack. At half past five, Sarah slipped out of her blue jeans and shirt and put on her ceremonial clothes. "It's time for me to return to the sacred circle," she announced.

Standing in the middle of the circle and facing west, she lit the long-stemmed pipe and repeated the acknowledgments to a spirit in heaven, a spirit in the earth, and other spirits in each of the four cardinal directions. At the moment the sun was about to disappear over the horizon, an arrow-shaped shadow briefly shot out from the cluster on the west side. Its tip touched Sarah's feet. She emptied the pipe's ashes into the small tin box, softly said something resembling a prayer, and stepped out of the circle.

It was September 21, the autumn equinox.

CHAPTER ELEVEN

Salt Lake City

*One's emotions, especially sudden, out-of-control emotions,
can cause a train wreck.*

Personal experience

When we got back to the pickup, I asked, "Do we have to return to Birney immediately? It's Friday tomorrow isn't it? We have the weekend in front of us"

"What would you like to do with it?"

"Eating would be a good start. Where is the closest place to find supper?"

"That would be Greybull. Go back to the junction and take a dogleg to the right."

That brought us to the precipice of the Bighorns. Greybull was not far away. But on that treacherous mountain road, distance was not measured in miles but in time. If I took one of the numerous switchbacks too fast, we'd get to Greybull quickly but not alive. Caution prevailed, and we eventually found ourselves at the bottom of a canyon. The canyon, in turn, molded into a valley with contours gentle enough for humanity to stake a claim. A sign—BLUEJACKETS SUPPER CLUB—caught my eye.

Bluejackets was a low-slung, ramshackle, ready-to-fall-in-on-itself building surrounded by beat-up pickups with rifles braced across their rear windows. Walking in, we were slapped in the face by the smell of cigarettes, beer, and steak. A menu-toting hostess, whose blouse was just barely up to the task for which it was intended, guided us to a table. At the back of the room, four loggers were shooting pool and doing some serious drinking. Sarah drew their attention immediately. That was hardly surprising. It probably had been a long time since any of them had been able to get within twenty feet of an attractive woman. As we took our seats at a table, the loggers wantonly stared at Sarah, slapped each other on the back, and made unheard but obviously lewd comments.

We were no more than seated when one of the loggers, a big, burly man with a four-inch scar running diagonally from his forehead and down over his eyebrow, headed toward the restroom. As the brute walked by our table, he pretended to stagger on his pool-table-sized legs and put his hands on our table to arrest his "fall." Slowly collecting himself, he ogled Sarah's breasts. I put a hand on his shoulder and went through the ritual of helping the behemoth resume a vertical posture. Irritated by the insinuation that he needed help, the logger glared at me with bloodshot eyes.

"You okay, Buddy?" I asked.

"Of course," he snorted and pushed himself upright. Turning his attention to Sarah, he flashed her a yellow-toothed, come-hither grin. She looked at the menu. Seeing that he was being ignored, the logger wobbled away. The stench he left behind consisted of more than chewing tobacco, booze, and body odor.

On returning to his pool game, the logger bumped against my shoulder, but he kept going. Approaching his cronies, he held two cupped hands over his chest and jiggled them up and down. The loggers snickered. Not content to leave it at that, the barbarian turned toward me and held two fingers behind the back of his head to indicate eagle feathers. He then brought his hands in front of him and curled the index finger of his left hand against his thumb, making a circle, and rapidly ran the middle finger of his right hand in and out of it. Laughing riotously, he saluted me with his middle finger.

"You bastard!" I called out, leaping to my feet.

Instantly, Sarah was in front of me. "Please take me out of here!" she said. I shoved her aside, and she fell back into her chair. But as I passed by her, Sarah grabbed my shirttail and hung on. "Please," she pleaded, "I don't want to be here."

In silence, we fled down the valley. Crossing the Bighorn River, we entered Greybull, Wyoming, population 1,953. Main Street was two blocks long; it took us to a T. We turned left at the stop sign, and Greybull was soon behind us.

"Thanks," I offered as we headed south.

"Thanks?"

"Thanks for keeping me out of Greybull's emergency room. That big bastard would have all but killed me. Is that a big problem out here?"

"Is what a problem?"

"Rednecks."

"Generally, not. We Indians can spot a redneck from a hundred yards, and we avoid them. But now and then there are problems."

"What kind of problems?"

"Like what happened a few years ago when a genial old man, but a bit of a drunk, was walking along the highway into Ashland. It was dusk. Two white cowboys came along in a pickup. They stopped and offered him a ride. When the Indian got one foot into the cab, the driver hit the accelerator. It flung the old man onto the road. The cowboys went on to the Club Buffet Bar in Ashland, where they bragged about what they had done to an Indian. What they did not know was that the old man was dead. He had hit his head on the asphalt, and it killed him. The cowboys were charged with manslaughter. At the trial, several witnesses testified they were in the bar and heard the cowboys brag about how they had tumbled an Indian into the ditch. The defense attorney claimed it was the Indian's drunkenness that caused him to fall out of the pickup and die. That was all the jury needed to hear. They found the cowboys not guilty."

"Why the animosity toward Indians?"

"Most of the local white ranchers think we stole the reservation from their ancestors. They also think it is their tax dollars that keeps the reservation going, conveniently forgetting about the millions of acres we ceded to the government for the promise of enough rations and annuities to keep us alive."

As we drove south, billboards began popping up, purporting that Worland, Wyoming, was the gateway to the Bighorns. The thought of encountering another redneck negated Worland's appeal for me. However, fifty yards farther down the highway another sign grabbed my interest. It read: WORLAND AIRPORT. I took a left and started down Worland's Main Street. When we passed by an acceptable-looking restaurant without stopping, Sarah flashed me a "Why not?" look. I smiled and kept driving. Coming to a street labeled "Airport Rd," I took it. In three miles, we came to the airport terminal, a small building squatting in the middle of a sagebrush flat. I parked and said, "Wait in the pickup a minute."

Hearing sounds in the lobby, a middle-aged woman came out of a small office in the back of the building. "Can I help ya?" she asked.

"What's the chance of catching a flight out this evening?"

"Ordinarily, you couldn't at this time of night. But the plane is three hours late coming out of Casper. Last year, it wouldn't have stopped here because there ain't no passengers tonight. Now, it stops, passengers or not. But it stops only long enough to drop off and pick up the airmail."

"Where's it going?"

"Salt Lake City."

Just then, a voice came on a scratchy radio. "That's them." Picking up a microphone, she related, "Wind's ten knots out of 2-8-0 favoring runway 3-4. Altimeter is three zero one four." Then, she went into the back office and, judging by the sounds of a shutting door, walked toward the runway. Soon, there was a loud KABOOM followed immediately by another KABOOM. Returning to the lobby, the woman propped a twelve-gauge shotgun in the corner. Seeing the mystified look on my face, she said, "Antelope. It gets 'em off the runway. Well, whatcha gonna do? If there ain't no passengers, that plane won't stay but long enough for us to exchange the mail."

"Two tickets to Salt Lake City," I said, sliding some cash across the counter, "and take ten out of it for yourself if you can do me a favor."

"What's the favor?" the woman asked apprehensively.

"Are you familiar with Salt Lake City?"

"Some."

"What's the nicest hotel right downtown?"

"That would be Hotel Utah."

"Could you phone Hotel Utah and make a reservation tonight for two? The name is Wagner, Jonathan Wagner." The woman nodded.

Hotel Utah sat smugly across the street from the Mormon Square. Bless the lady at the Worland Airport, the clerk had our reservation, and we had a room. In the lobby, a well-dressed man waited for the elevator. When the door opened, several couples emerged. No one smirked. No one leered. No one made an obscene gesture. It was nice to be back in civilization.

As we entered our hotel room, I put an arm around Sarah, and she pressed her head against my shoulder. "It feels good to be here, doesn't it?" I commented.

"No, it doesn't!"

"It doesn't? What's wrong?"

"I was hungry six hours ago. Now I'm famished. Could we at least get a sandwich?"

"Sure. You take a hot bath, and I'll find us something to eat."

Taking the elevator down to the lobby, I approached the hotel clerk and asked, "Is it possible to get a couple of sandwiches, some bubble bath, and a bottle of champagne?"

"Sandwiches are no problem. Bubble bath can be obtained, but champagne; that's another matter. Especially here!" he said, casting his eyes upward as if the God of temperance lived on the top floor. "This is an LDS town. There is no place at this time of night where YOU could get champagne. But I could possibly procure a bottle for you." We struck a deal. When in Rome, do as the Romans do. When in Salt Lake City, expect to pay dearly for a bottle of champagne.

When I got back to the room, Sarah was drawing a bath. I knocked on the bathroom door.

"Yes?" she replied apprehensively.

"May I come in?"

"Wait a minute!" The water stopped. Bare feet squeaked on the tile floor. Then it was quiet. "Okay," she said.

Sarah was up to her neck in a bathtub full of hot water. Seeing that I had a sandwich, she eagerly reached for it. She also noticed that I was holding my left hand behind my back, hiding something.

"And?" she asked, flashing a bemused smile.

Covertly setting the bottle of champagne on the floor behind me, I did my best imitation of a magician's sleight of hand to present a bottle of bubble bath. Opening the bottle, I slowly poured its contents along her legs and used my hand to stir up a stream of bubbles. Standing, I took off my shirt and unbuckled my belt.

"Welcome to my little corner of the world," she said.

Once settled in the front of the bathtub, I revealed the bottle of champagne that I had covertly slid up tight against the side of the bathtub.

"There are two kinds of Indians," Sarah responded solemnly. "There are Indians who shouldn't drink, and there are Indians who don't drink. I belong to the latter band."

"Of course," I said, setting the champagne down.

When I woke in the morning, Sarah was at the window looking out at the snow-capped Wasatch Range. A stack of pamphlets was in her lap. She was dressed and ready to attack the city. Grabbing bagels and coffee at a corner deli, we struck out for the Beehive, the first stop on her list of attractions. As we entered the Beehive, Sarah said, "Did you know Brigham Young had twenty-seven wives? One of them was only fifteen years old, and most of them were in their twenties."

"Is it too late for me to become a Mormon?"

"Don't get any unhealthy ideas from these strange white people."

"What makes you think their ideas are unhealthy?"

"They'd be unhealthy for you. My knife is sharp, and I'd use it to remove more than your scalp."

"Yea, though I walk through the Valley of Mormons, I will think no evil."

"Epeva'e!"

That day, we did the tourist thing. We saw the Beehive, toured the Mormon Square with its daunting cathedral and oval-shaped assembly hall, and ate lunch at a sidewalk café. After lunch, we went for a touristy stroll through the business district. As we walked by the Hansen Planetarium, a bill-board caught Sarah's attention: *Mr. Einstein's Universe*. Sarah wanted to see it. I was certain she had no clue what the movie was about; nonetheless, I bought two tickets.

As we walked out of the movie and into the bright light of day, Sarah was unusually quiet. Undoubtedly, she found the movie hard to follow and not what she expected.

"That was a great movie," she finally exclaimed. "Isn't it interesting that Newton's three laws of motion intuitively make sense and the mathematics of it are simple, concise, and straightforward? Then along comes Einstein. He upsets the apple cart by telling us things about our universe that are not intuitive and are almost impossible to comprehend. Things like space is curved; there are places in the universe where time goes faster than other places; and how a person sees a particular event depends on where the observer is standing. The universe that Einstein revealed is downright dumbfounding, at least to me."

My jaw dropped. "Where did you learn so much about Newton and Einstein?"

"I read a book once. Hey," she said, pointing up the street, "here comes the bus that goes to Snowbird. I think it stops at the corner. If we run, we can catch it."

Sunday afternoon, we flew back to Worland. As the plane descended into the Bighorn River Valley, my mind reviewed our delightful weekend in Salt Lake City. "Wouldn't you like to live there?" I asked.

"Live where?"

"In Salt Lake City, you and me?"

"Nope."

Chapter Twelve

A Matter of Values

*"We do not want riches. Riches would do us no good.
We cannot take them with us to the other world.
We only want peace and love."*

Chief Red Cloud, Oglala Sioux

After lunch on Monday, Joe and I propped ourselves at our reserved places against the south foundation to soak up the sun. Before Joe could say a word, he had to have a smoke. When nicotine was coursing through his blood, he was ready for a confab. "Nice day, eh?," he said.

"Joe, what's it like living here year end and year out?"

"Well, livin' here has its sunny parts, and it has its parts that stick in your craw."

"What are the sunny parts?"

"Ya see it right there," Joe replied, sweeping his arm across the horizon. "This is the most beautiful place in the world. But that's not what ya mean, is it."

"No. Not exactly."

"Well, the sunny parts would be the Cheyenne people. They are a good people. They are honest and kind. There aren't many fights and very few killin's unless there is alcohol around. What I take a fancy to is that life here is slow. Ya can sit back and enjoy it. If ya learn to appreciate those little things, then life on the rez is good."

"And the things that stick in your craw. What would they be?"

"Bein' poor. There ain't no money on the rez except the welfare checks the government gives out every month. The welfare checks are barely enough to keep people from starvin' to death. Then ya have to remember that the government money is free. Nobody on the rez earned it, and that brings problems of its own."

At that, Joe fell silent. It was typical Joe. He delighted in eliciting my curiosity and then falling silent until I provided the prompt to continue that he was looking for.

"And what are those problems?"

"The problem is that when the money is free, nobody takes care of notin'. Take when I was a kid on the Turtle Mountain Rez. We'd sometimes go to Devils Lake fer Saturday night shoppin'. Like as not, there would be a Belcourt school bus drivin' around Devils Lake. The bus driver either had a reason to go to Devils Lake or his relative did, but neither of 'em had a way to get there. So, they take the school bus. Nobody says notin'. Why should they? Nobody on the rez bought the bus. Nobody on the rez paid for the gas. It's the government's bus burnin' up the government's gas. Do you want to know what else I think?

"Definitely."

"I think that all of us on the rez should pay a little bit of tax to help pay for our schools, tribal police, medical clinic, and the like. Then we might take better care of them."

"I have another question for you, Joe. I've heard that more than half of the Cheyenne live in poverty. What keeps them in poverty?"

"You heard it was half? Hell, it's more like eighty percent. And if ya figure out what can be done about it, why they might just elect ya the tribal chairman.

At that, Joe stopped talking while he got out the makings to roll a cigarette. When the cigarette was rolled and lit, and Joe had some nicotine in this blood, he continued. "In truth, I don't know the answer, but I knows it has somethin' ta do with Indian crabs.

"Indian crabs? What do Indian crabs have to do with poverty?"

"Well, there were three fellers walkin' on along the Oregon coast diggin' fer crabs. One was a Scotchman, the other was a German, and the third one was an Indian. All three of them were diggin' crabs and puttin' them in their buckets. After an hour, the tide came in, and they had to quit. Each of them looks in his bucket to count his crabs. The German was surprised. He had only three crabs in his bucket, and one of them was about to get out. The Scotchman was more surprised. He had only one crab in his bucket. Then they look in the Indian's bucket, and they were really surprised. The Indian's bucket was full of crabs. 'How come is it,' The Scotchman said to the Indian, that the crabs climbed out of our buckets, but no crabs shinnied out of yours?'

"'It's because I pick only Indian crabs.'

'Indian crabs?' the German said. 'What's so special about Indian crabs?'

'If Indian crabs see another Indian crab gettin' up above them, they reach up and pull that Indian crab back down.'"

"Joe, have you seen that happening?"

"Have I seen it happening? Hell, its happened to me over and over. Take last year. Maggie has a relative who tried to make it off the rez on one of them government relocation programs. He got a job in Denver, workin' in a plant. His job was putting four screws into the top of a water pump and passin' it to the next guy down the line. They paid him two and a half bucks an hour. He soon found out ya can't live in Denver on no two and a half bucks an hour. So, back he comes to the rez. But his car broke down near Wheatland, Wyomin'.He was a week hitchhiking back here. When he got dumped off in Ashland, the first place he stuck out for was our house. I mean to tell ya, he was a sorry sight. He was hungry, dirty, smelly, and broke. But like I said, he is some relation to Maggie; so, we took him in. He stayed us for a month and darn near ate us out of house and home. I had an old car sittin' around. It wasn't much, but it ran. To get rid of him, I gave him the car, and Maggie gave him fifty bucks, all her savin's. But if ya can stick it out, you get use to it. First thing ya know, it feels good. Ya got enough money to get by. And what difference does it make if I drive my fifteen-year-old pickup or a brand new one like yours, eh? Besides, my old pickup has something yours don't."

He stopped to take a long drag on his cigarette, again making it necessary for me to tug on the dangling hook.

"What would that be?"

"When my pickup breaks down 'tween my place and town, I have an excuse to stop at my Indian relative's house and eat some of his grub," Joe snickered, giving himself that congratulatory slap on the leg.

A few evenings later, Sarah and I took a walk after school. Joe's explanation of why so many Cheyenne lived in poverty was still on my mind. "Sarah, have you ever heard of Indian crabs?"

"So, Joe told you that story, did he? He loves to tell it to anyone who will sit long enough to listen."

"Is there any truth to it?"

"Joe isn't an Indian. He's Métis, a race and a culture all their own. He was born and for the most part reared on the Turtle Mountain Reservation in North Dakota. He has never traveled east of North Dakota in his entire life or west beyond the Bighorn Mountains. Joe's Indian crab story is his attempt to make sense of the small world he has known."

"So, the Indian crab story has no basis?"

"Maybe a little, but only a little."

"And?"

"And what?"

"And what is the part of the story Joe is missing?"

"This is a nice evening. The meadowlarks are saying goodbye to the setting sun, the Tongue River is laughing as it flows toward the Yellowstone, the coyotes will soon be greeting the evening stars, and you want to talk about Indian crabs?"

"Well, I want to know why Joe thinks the Northern Cheyenne keep pulling each other down."

"For Whitemen, the world is all about making money and, as they put it, getting ahead. Their cultural heroes are rich white folk, and they don't care what the person did to get rich. Take the wealthiest man in America in his day, John Jacob Aster. He added to his wealth by plotting with England against America. Then there was John D. Rockefeller. When the coal miners in Ludlow, Colorado, wanted to be paid a little more so they could feed their families and give them a better place to live than a tent, they went on strike. Did Rockefeller, the wealthiest man in America, pull out his thick wallet and give them a few more cents an hour? No, he didn't. Rockefeller brought in the National Guard. The soldiers fired machine guns into the workers' tent encampment, killing men, women, and children. As for Andrew Carnegie, when the steel mill workers went on strike, he stood by quietly while the Pinkerton detectives and the state militia waged gun battles with his underpaid workers. Those are but three examples out of the thousands of cases in which rich white folk made vast amounts of money by scheming against their country, keeping workers' wages down, and doing things they knew would put their laborers in an early grave. It still goes on. For Whitemen, the pursuit of money is a religion.

"Joe's Indian crab joke, as he calls it, has it all wrong. It is not that one Indian pulls another down. Rather, every Indian is willing to help a fellow Cheyenne get back on his feet. In the old days, we chose our chiefs by considering who had shown exceptional willingness and ability to help the less fortunate. If a hard winter came along and little game could be found, our bravest and strongest men traveled far to find game. When they found it, they brought the meat back to camp and shared it with those who were hungry. In the old days, a Cheyenne gave his food, his buffalo hides, and even his horses to those in need. He gave what he had until he had no more or even less than his kinsmen. Today, helping the less fortunate continues to be the Cheyenne way. We are generous, giving people. Unfortunately, nearly all of us are poor. When we give away what little we have, we have next to nothing. Soon, all of us are poor. But we'd rather live in poverty than be like rich white folk who make money off the backs of poor, working people."

CHAPTER THIRTEEN

Trying to See Down the Road

Listen, or your tongue will make you deaf.

Whereas the Northern Cheyenne Reservation is not vast, it is intriguing—full of mystery and surprises. During the weekends, Sarah and I often made excursions to its unique, awesome places. Two aspects of our outings were predictable. One constant was our conversation. We mostly talked about the sights, sounds, aromas, and other things brought to us by our senses. Any attempts I made, be they direct or subtle, to learn even small details of Sarah's earlier life were either ignored or answered with a new topic. In return, Sarah never asked about my past. She acted as if the path that brought me into her life did not matter. Come to think about it, maybe it didn't.

The other predictable was the food. Whatever food Sarah pulled from her rucksack came the way nature provided it—a baked potato; an ear of corn, either roasted or raw; a carrot, always raw; or an apple. Meat was a staple. Sometimes, it was jerky, the traditional kind, meaning venison or antelope cut into thin slices and smoked in just enough heat to make it hard and dry but surprisingly tasty. If the meat came from a smaller creature, its anatomical relation to the animal was never in doubt. We ate breast of grouse, leg of rabbit, wing of duck. Sarah never reached into her rucksack and produced a muffin, a piece of homemade bread, a leftover pancake, or anything composed of ingredients and the result of what could be called baking.

There was another commonality about our excursions. They

always ended where they began, the school. Sarah politely refused my invitations to show her my camp on Poker Jim Creek. Likewise, she never offered to take me to her house. All I knew was that she lived along the Birney Road that ran north along the west side of the Tongue River. Where she lived seemed to be a carefully guarded secret. If Sarah shared a house with anyone, she did not seem to have any caretaking responsibilities because our time together ended when it reached a natural conclusion. But if Sarah resided alone, why was she so secretive? Perhaps her house was located amidst a cluster of homes, and if she brought a man home, it would set many tongues wagging. Or was there another reason?

What wasn't predictable about our excursions was the destinations. Sarah always had a different place in mind. The magic of these destinations was obvious. One memorable outing was the time we hiked up a draw that led to Section Line Spring. Upon nearing the spring, we lay among the sagebrush, waiting and watching as the evening unfolded. It was not long before mule deer came out of the hills, sometimes alone, but often in groups of two or three. The deer trailed down the draw leading to the spring. Some of them walked within a few yards of us. Particularly touching were a doe and her fawn who stopped along the top of the nearby ridge where the doe suckled its fawn in the light of the setting sun.

There were things that, if alone, I would not have seen. One such occurrence was when we drove along the road—more of a jeep trail—that led up Pawnee Creek. Along the way, we passed a gulch whose mouth opened onto the creek. At the face of the gulch was a limestone rock approximately six feet long and five feet high. As we drove past it, Sarah pointed to the rock escarpment and said, "That's a coyote howl."

"What do you mean, a coyote howl?'"

"That's where a coyote comes at sunset to howl."

"How do you know that? Have you seen a coyote go there in the evening to howl?"

"No, but I know it is a coyote howl because there is a well-used animal path that leads to the rock face and look at the contour of the rock. Its shape is parabolic. Like a bandstand in a city park, it amplifies the coyote's howl and sends it booming into the valley."

"You are making this coyote into an acoustical engineer."

"I suppose I have to show you!"

"Yes. You have created a 'I-have-to-see-it-to-believe-it moment.'"

"Okay. I'll do that. But we'll have to wait a few days. The coyote has noticed our intrusion into his territory. He will be vigilant and not likely to return to his regular comings and goings for a while.

The next weekend we drove up Pawnee Creek about an hour before sunset. We parked a mile away from the so-called coyote howl and walked up the valley. When we were within two hundred yards of the parabolically shaped rock, Sarah motioned that we should hide behind some tall sagebrush.

We lay silent and motionless for a half hour, but nothing appeared other than a mountain bluebird who flitted from bush to bush. After another ten minutes of silence, we heard a coyote howl. But the howl did not come from anywhere near the gulch. It came from far up Pawnee Creek. To add insult to injury, a coyote started yipping up a storm between us and my pickup. By then, the sun was sliding toward its demise, and shadows were creeping into the valley. Victory would soon be mine.

Just as a smirk was finding its way to my face, Sarah's foot touched my leg. She caught my eyes with hers and cast my attention toward the so-called coyote howl. A huge coyote emerged from the brush at the bottom of the gulch and climbed the side of the outcropping to the base of the parabolically shaped rock. But when the animal reached the acclaimed coyote howl, he did not howl. Instead, he sat down on his haunches and surveyed the valley. The rock outcropping wasn't a coyote howl. It was his watchtower. As the sun began to disappear behind the Wolf Mountains, the coyote stood on all fours and stretched. My smirk morphed into a smile. But at that moment, the damn animal tilted back his head and let go with a howl that boomed out of the gulch like a cannon blast. All the coyotes in the valley frenetically answered.

Another memorable excursion was a trip to the plateau that marks the divide between the Birney Day School and Lame Deer. To this day, what transpired there plays and replays in my mind.

It was a Sunday morning, and we met at the school. Sarah

jumped into my pickup and directed me to take the Lame Deer Road, which led us past successive stands of cottonwood, box elder, and ash. As we gradually ascended the divide, the deciduous trees gave way to ponderosa pine. When the road quit climbing, we were on the top of a forested plateau. There was a logging road to our left. Sarah gestured to take it. When we had gone about three miles down it, she said, "Stop. Let's walk."

The countryside was inviting. Meadows, still showing a tint of green despite the lateness of the season, were delightfully interspersed among stands of tall pine. "It's beautiful," I sighed.

"You should see it in its Sunday clothes."

"Sunday clothes?"

"Mother Earth puts on her Sunday clothes in the spring. No sooner does the snow melt than pasques bravely reach out to the world with its lavender flowers. As spring advances, the pasques follow the snow's retreat, wrapping the north side of the plateau in a purple ribbon. Then along comes a particularly warm day whose breath lingers through the night, gently caressing the chokecherry and plum trees in the lower valley until they burst out in flowers that punctuate the hillsides with clusters of white. Still, spring does not quit. As its last pronouncement, yellow snapdragons pop up to catch a glint of the sun, and lupine adorn the shady spots with bell-shaped blue flowers. In the spring, this is my favorite place on the reservation."

"I'd love to see this plateau when it is a carpet of flowers. We must come back here next spring"

Rather endorsing the idea or even giving a confirming smile, Sarah broke into a long stride that put physical and emotional distance between us, and it seemed intentional. "Sarah!" I called out, as she walked away from me, "Are you worried that one of these days I might leave?"

Throwing her words over her shoulder, she replied, "Leave? I never gave it any thought. "Are you wanting to leave?"

"No!"

"Look at this!" she exclaimed, stopping to kneel beside a tall sagebrush. "Last spring, a pair of wrens wove this nest into the branches of this bush." Taking her knife out of the pocket of her blue jeans, she cut off the thick, fibrous branches holding the nest. "Isn't this little nest beautiful? The kids at school will love it."

Needing to find a way out of the emotional minefield into which I had led us, I asked, "Won't the wren come looking for its nest next spring?"

"No. Wrens, like all songbirds, build a new nest every spring. Birds carry lice and mites that lay eggs in the bird's nest. If the wren used the same nest next spring, the lice and mites in the nest would devour the hatchlings. In the old times, the Cheyenne lived like the birds, always moving to a new nest. That kept us healthy and strong. But when white hunters killed off the buffalo and the government confined us to reservations, the Indian Department set up ration stations where they handed out spoiled food and barely enough to keep us from starving to death. In time, The People built log cabins near the ration stations. The cabins had only a few tiny windows that let light in but could not be opened to admit fresh air. The cabins had no running water and were heated by wood-burning stoves. They were hothouses for disease. An influenza epidemic swept through the reservation in 1919, killing hundreds of Cheyenne. But the flu was kind. Its victims either got well, or they died in a few days. Tuberculosis also lived among us, and it wasn't kind. At first, those who were infected with TB did not feel well. It was like having a cold that won't go away. Six months later they were spitting up heavy, gray phlegm. Within a year or two, the phlegm was tinged with blood. They died from the inside out, taking a long time to do it. TB killed lots of Cheyenne."

As Sarah talked about birds, influenza, and tuberculosis, her unwillingness to talk about our future tortured my mind and wouldn't let go. Why was she consistently unwilling to talk about our future? Maybe my skin was the wrong color, and Sarah had no intention of diluting her Cheyenne heritage with mixed-blood children.

"Sarah," I blurted out, "how would you feel about raising mixed-blood children?"

"Whose children?"

"Ours!"

"You want to have children?" she asked, raising a skeptical eyebrow.

"No. Not right now. But what if I did? How would you feel about it?"

"When you are ready to become a father, ask me then."

After traipsing along the ridge for an hour, we came upon an outcropping of limestone that jutted out of the plateau like a thumb. We sat on the edge of the outcropping and dangled our legs over the edge. Digging into her rucksack, Sarah produced an apple and two bottles of Coke. Without saying a word, she handed me a bottle of Coke, cut the apple in two, and handed half of it to me. We ate in silence. I decided that she had created this riff, and it was her problem to solve. So, I vowed to myself that I would not be the first to talk.

To divert my attention, I scanned the country below us. The rounded hills of hard clay and shale grabbed my attention and dredged up what I remembered from a college geology class taken years ago. I realized that the hills' horizontal bands of faded gray and drab red were vestiges of the Cretaceous Sea, a vast body of water that, a hundred million years ago, covered the land from Gulf of Mexico to the Arctic Ocean and split the landmass of the American Continent in two. Sixty million years ago, the Laramie Orogeny pushed the land up, drained away the inland sea, and thrust the Bighorn Mountains into the landscape. The sediment at the bottom of the Cretaceous Sea eventually hardened, forming the limestone that now caps the plateau in southeast Montana, such as the one on which we were sitting. Looking down the long valley, I saw, here and there, red rocks laced with black streaks which suggested the area was once assaulted from below by protrusions of lava. It was not. Thirty million years ago, the coal seams that lace through southeastern corner of Montana were more exposed than they are today. When the exposed coal seams were struck by lightning, they occasionally ignited and sometimes burned hot enough to melt the adjacent sedimentary rock, which cooled into the red rocks that are now called "clinkers."

Looking closer by, I noticed a small mound of rocks roughly seven feet long and two feet high. It had the appearance of having been placed there by intent. Forgetting my covertly made vow of silence, I pointed toward the pile of rocks and asked, "What's that?"

Sarah's eyes followed my extended arm to the pile of rocks. "It's a grave. We must go." Like trespassers, we quietly sneaked away. When we were out of earshot of the grave, Sarah explained what we had seen. "In the old days, we buried our deceased along the tops of ridges like this one. Beside the body, mourners placed objects the person might need in the next life, like a favorite bow, good arrows, a war club, jerky, and always the person's medicine pouch. They covered the body and those things with stones too heavy for a predatory animal to dislodge but fitted loosely so the person's spirit could escape and travel the Milky Way to Seyan. When the government put us on the rez and under the thumb of Indian agents, the agents scolded us for being pagans and ordered us to bury our dead in the ground, and then only in a cemetery beside a Whiteman church. For a time, we refused to obey and continued to bury our dead in the old way. But no longer. Now all deceased Cheyenne get buried just like a white man, whether they want to be or not."

While Sarah was telling me about traditional Cheyenne burials, we walked in a clockwise circle that brought us to the pickup. As we drove back to the school, the sun slipped below the horizon, and Sarah put her head on my shoulder and fell asleep. While she slept, my mind returned to issue that was still upsetting me: Why did Sarah consistently refuse to talk about anything that put the two of us together in the future. Was she unwilling to discuss our future because I was nothing more than a timely and convenient diversion? Were there things about me that annoyed her so much she wouldn't be tolerating me much longer? Or was she unwilling to discuss our future because I wasn't a Northern Cheyenne? Those questions nagged at me, grabbed hold, and wouldn't let go.

CHAPTER FOURTEEN

Billings, Montana

*"In this life, a man should be so lucky as to have
one good horse and one good woman."*

Wisdom from an old cowboy in Worden, Montana

Upon arriving at school day morning, I was surprised to see a big Buick in the parking lot. The children were out for recess. Instead of being at the lunch table having their gab session, every teacher was on the playground monitoring her wards. Sarah was nowhere to be seen. Maggie and her helper, Dawn, were in the kitchen. I found Joe in his workroom and asked him what was up with the Buick in the parking lot."

"It's the bossman's," he whispered, rolling his eyes upward toward the classrooms.

"The bossman? Who's that?"

"Arneson. He's out of the BIA office in Billings and is the school principal. He comes down here every now and again to check up on things. Everyone here gives him the stink eye. If we are lucky, it'll be a tough winter, and we won't see his face again until green grass comes."

"Isn't Sarah the principal?"

"You have to have degrees and titles to get the big bucks. Sarah ain't got none of those. She's just the secretary. Now get out of here and stay away until that Buick is gone, and that might be a couple of days."

Being temporarily banished from the school offered me the opportunity to go in search of something that might prove useful should Sarah and I make another overnight excursion. That necessitated a 150-mile trip to the largest town Montana had to offer.

Billings, Montana, was a dirty-around-the-collar town with the aspiration to be bigger than it was. The town got its start when the Northern Pacific Railroad, coming from Minneapolis and bound for Seattle, laid its tracks up the Yellowstone River Valley in 1882 and built a series of station stops along the tracks. Those 'stops' were nothing more than places to get water for the steam-powered locomotives and, depending on the location, to load up with coal or wood for the boiler. One of those stops was dubbed Billings, in honor of the then-president of the Northern Pacific Railroad, Frederick H. Billings. When Billings was still a pup, it stood on its hind legs and peered over the sagebrush, trying to see if its future might be coming on the next train. It heard the mooing of cattle and the bleating of sheep. Big operators came to Billings and put thousands of cattle and sheep on the grass-covered plateau that stretched north of Billings clear to the Canadian border. Each fall, market-ready livestock were herded into the stockyard at the east end of town, loaded into stockcars, and shipped to slaughterhouses in Chicago. But the hot, dry summer of 1886 took the bloom off that rose, and the winter of 1886-1887 killed it. Snow came early that November and ushered in extreme cold. By December, snow lay heavy on the prairie, and relentless winds prowled the landscape. When spring finally showed its face in May of 1887, herds that had once numbered in the thousands were less than a hundred. The winter of 1886-1887 taught the big operators that nineteen out of twenty winters on the Northern Great Plains were reasonably open. The snow depth could be measured in inches, the January thaw arrived on schedule, and cattle and sheep could be profitably raised. But every decade or two, the Northern Great Plains churn up blizzards that devastate entire herds. Now, less than a hundred years later, the rails that led to the livestock yard were rusted, and weeds were growing up between the ties. The dream of cattle empires on the Northern Great Plains was dead.

At the north edge of Billings, a small college sat under an outcrop of red rimrock. Everything about the campus announced that higher education was not going to put the wannabe city on the map.

If the adolescent town was going to amount to anything, its growth would come from a four-story building at the northeast edge of the business district. The building had enough glass to give it that all-important modern look and sufficient concrete to announce that its feet were planted on bedrock. Big letters above the door said it all in one word: PETROLEUM. Billings was betting its future on oil refining.

But it was not the railroad, cattle empires, the institution of higher learning, or oil refining that brought me to Billings. I came to town to buy a tent, one of the latest designs being advertised in catalogs, a tent made of lightweight, closely woven nylon.

Advertising is a fantastic thing. It makes you want what you cannot get. When I asked about a backpacker's tent at the Coast-to-Coast store in Billings, the clerk said, "Sure, we have a good selection." Then he tried to sell me a scaled-down version of my heavy, canvas wall-tent. At another store, the clerk was more honest. "Never heard of such a thing," she replied. A customer overheard us and suggested the Gamble Store in Laurel might have a backpacker's tent. "It's but thirteen miles to the west," he said.

The owner of the Gamble store in Laurel was a tall, slender man whose bright eyes peered out at the world from beneath ready-to-take-flight eyebrows. Harold Remington had a salesman's ready smile, and he had something more important than that. He had a backpacker's tent.

The Northern, a big hotel in the middle of Billings, promised a much-appreciated luxury: a hot bath. Thoroughly cleansed, a soft bed beckoned.

Tuesday morning, hunger catapulted me across the street to Sambo's Restaurant. There, a day-old newspaper and French toast of the same vintage were consumed. It was time to say goodbye to Billings.

Taking a different and only slightly longer route back to Poker Jim Creek brought me to Worden, Montana, a little town thirty miles east of Billings. Tucked into a bend of the Yellowstone River, the town seemed to wish time would pass it by. Its wish had been pretty much granted. Replace the half-dozen vehicles parked along Main Street with horses and buggies and remove the electric power poles, you'd have Worden, Montana, circa 1890. A quick trip around town revealed there was not much to the town, but there was one thing that interested me. Behind a small house on the edge of town lay a pile of weathered 1 x 10 rough-cut lumber. Presumably, someone had bought the lumber to build something. Like many aspirations, this one was long on intent but short on effort. The weathered lumber was a fortuitous find. A few 1 x 10s, if they could be bought cheaply, would make nice skirting for my wall tent on Poker Jim Creek.

In response to a knock on the door, an old man answered. Despite his age, which was at least eighty, he was narrow at the hip, broad at the shoulder, and as straight as an arrow. His hands were calloused and gnarled from a lifetime of use. He was only about five feet seven inches, but the two-inch heels on his cowboy boots gave him the appearance of height. He looked long and hard at me as his tongue escorted chewing tobacco from one side of his mouth to the other. When he had sized me up, the old codger spat a humongous glob of dark juice over my left shoulder and in a querulous tone asked, "And just what is it ya want, Sonny?"

"Are you the owner of the pile of lumber out back?"

"You been pokin' around my place, have ya?" he challenged.

"No Sir. The lumber is quite visible from the street. It looks like it has been laying there for a while, and it seemed you might be willing to sell some of it."

"Who ya representin'?"

"I'm not representing anybody!"

To ensure I was telling the truth, he stuck his head out the door and looked up and down the street. "Is that your outfit?" he asked, referring to the only vehicle in sight.

"Yes Sir."

"You ain't no religious nut, are ya?" he asked, raising his hand like he'd cuff me if I was a proselytizer.

"I just want to buy a few pieces of lumber."

With that assurance, his gruff demeanor evaporated. "Come in," he said, disappearing into the bowels of his dark, little house.

Four steps took us into a small kitchen where, at the sink, flies feasted on a plate of day-old beans. A cat sat on the windowsill, basking in the afternoon sun. Seeing me, it hissed and then escaped through the open window.

"Sit yourself, Sonny," the old man said, taking two coffee cups out of the cupboard. Giving the cups a quick inspection, he pulled his shirttail out of his pants and used it to wipe away the dirt and smudges on the inside of the cups. Grabbing a coffee pot off the wood-burning stove, he poured two cups and slid one in front of me. "You're interested in my lumber, are ya?"

"Yes, if the price is not too high."

"Ya see, I bought that lumber to be a shed for Buck," the old man said as he took a seat in the chair on the other side of the wooden table. "You've probably heard of Buck. He was the best cow horse in the Yellowstone Valley. Everybody wanted to buy him. I mean to tell ya, some of them big ole ranchers wanted Buck so bad that they'd roll up a gob of money and try to stick it in my shirt pocket. But I just stepped back and left 'em holding their money. To my way of thinking, every man in his life deserves one good horse and one good woman. I've been lucky; I've had both."

"How true," I sighed.

Thinking I was a fellow equine philosopher, he smiled, but looking at my feet and not seeing pointy-toed boots with two-inch heels a frown came over his face. He spit a salvo of tobacco juice into a Folgers coffee-can sitting beside the table. Relieved of a mouthful of tobacco juice, he continued. "Believe me, Sonny, them big ranchers would've paid any price I named for Buck. But, like I said, Buck wasn't for sale. When Buck got older, the winters started to get to him. Even down here along the river, it can get downright cold. So, I made a trip all the way to Wyomin' to buy lumber so I could build a shed for Buck. Ya know, don't ya," he said, putting on a used-car-salesman's air, "that weatherin' don't do a thing to lumber but cure it. That lumber is as good as the day it was sawed from a log, maybe better. I bought that lumber in August, and wouldn't ya know, Buck ups and dies before the first snowflake fell."

Between the old man's sentimental attachment to the lumber and his ability to make a sales pitch, the price he wanted for a few pieces of rough-cut, wasting-away lumber was likely climbing to astronomical proportions.

He sat in his chair for a long moment, sipping his coffee and looking through the window at the stack of lumber. "How much of it do ya want?"

"Only eight pieces. What would be a fair price?"

"Just take 'em," he replied, not bothering to look at me.

"No. That wouldn't be fair."

The old cowboy didn't respond because he was looking out the window at a horse only he could see. Leaving a twenty-dollar bill under my coffee cup, I tiptoed out of his life.

It was late afternoon when I got back to the Birney Day School. School was out, and everyone was gone. A key in my glove compartment opened the door to the school. A search of Joe's workroom uncovered a shovel, a saw, a hammer, and some ten-penny nails. I drove back to my camp on Poker Jim Creek and began sawing the 1 x 10s to length and digging a four-inch-deep trench around the tent. I placed one set of boards in the trench so that the bottom of the tent draped over it and then placed matching boards outside of the draped-over portion of the tent. After the boards were nailed at the corners and dirt shoveled against them, the job was finished. The next cold wind that crawled around my tent would come face to face with a no-trespassing sign.

That being done, I stretched out on my army cot and tried to go to sleep. As I lay there in the dark, the wizened words of Buck's owner tumbled through my mind: "To my way of thinking, every man in his life deserves one good horse and one good woman. I've been lucky; I've had both. "

I hoped to become as lucky as that old cowboy.

CHAPTER FIFTEEN

Lisa conquers her Mountain.

"Once you learn to read, you will be forever free."

Frederick Douglas

Wednesday morning, the Buick was gone, making it safe for me to stick my head in the basement door. Lisa was not at the lunchroom table waiting for her reading lesson, so Maggie went upstairs to fetch her. When Lisa emerged from the stairs, she timidly edged toward our lunch-room table and sat down with painfully obvious reluctance. I began to read: "Dolphins live in all seven oceans of the world . . ." As I read, Lisa's eyes followed my finger as it moved from word to word. After five minutes of reading, I put my finger under the word 'dolphin' and said, "Lisa, what's the first letter of this word?"

"D"

"Do you know what sound a 'd' makes?"

"duh."

"That's right!"

I asked her to identify other letters in the word and say their sound. Lisa knew the names of all the letters and the sound associated with each. As a real reading teacher would put it, she knew the letter symbol–letter sounds associations.

When Lisa came in from morning recess, we resumed reading the dolphin book. When we were well into the lesson and Lisa was comfortably engaged, I put my finger under the word "sand" and said, "Lisa, look at each letter, say its sound, and then tell me the word."

" 'S' as in s."

"Very good, and now for the rest of the letters in the word."

" 'A' as in ah, 'n' as in nn, 'd' as in duh."

"Very good, and what is the word?"

Putting her finger under each letter, Lisa again said, though somewhat louder, " 'S' as in ss 'a' as in ah, 'n' as in nn, 'd' as in duh."

"Right. And what word do the sounds say when you put the sounds together?" Lisa didn't say anything, and a terrified look came over her face. "The word is sand," I said.

Lisa whispered, "I don't want to read anymore," and she fled up the stairs.

Within minutes, Sarah came down from her office. Before she could say anything, I said, "I'm the wrong person to teach Lisa to read. You need to get someone else."

"All toddlers fall with their first step. You'll figure it out."

When the noon recess was over and the other students had gone to their classrooms, Lisa entered the lunchroom and stood in the doorway, frozen. Mrs. Fighting Bear immediately came out of the kitchen with a dish of ice cream covered with chocolate syrup. The gruff, old cook handed the bowl of ice cream to Lisa, guided the little waif to the lunchroom table, and sat beside her. As Lisa scrunched herself tightly against Mrs. Fighting Bear and ate ice cream, I began reading a book about tigers. It wasn't long until Lisa's eyes began to follow my finger as it slid from word to word.

That was our final reading lesson of the day. The lesson did nothing that helped Lisa learn to read, but it accomplished one thing. When Lisa left the reading session, she was not crushed and disheartened.

It was clear to me that a phonetic approach to teaching Lisa to read wouldn't work. It wasn't that Lisa lacked the ability to use phonics. In the hands of a competent reading teacher, Lisa undoubtedly could have quickly learned to decode words phonetically. But my ignorant, uninformed, and downright stupid attempt to teach her how to sound out words had ignited within her a deep-seated sense of failure.

When Lisa came down the stairs Tuesday morning, I had another approach in mind. "Lisa, do you have any pets?"

"I have a dog."

"What do you call your dog?"

"Sam."

"What is Sam good for? What does he do?"

"Mostly, Sam sleeps by the door, but he wakes up and barks whenever somebody comes. At night, he scares away the coons and the skunks. Grandma says that when it gets cold, Sam can come in the house, sleep on my bed, and keep me warm."

That morning, Lisa told me about her grandmother, the new friends she was making at school, the games she likes to play at recess, and many other things that made up her world. When the reading lesson ended and Lisa returned to class, she climbed the steps with lighter feet.

While the children were at morning recess, I prepared twelve cards, each with a different word. The words related to things Lisa had told me about that morning: Sam, dog, his, name, is, house, I, have, lives, at, like. When Lisa came in for her second reading lesson, I showed her the first card—Sam. "This word is Sam, the name of your dog. Say the word and then draw a picture of Sam on the card." Like most Cheyenne children, Lisa had a flair for drawing. She quickly sketched a picture of Sam.

"This card says dog. Draw a picture of a dog, any dog but Sam." Lisa sketched the typical reservation dog, smaller than Sam and with short, pointed ears. She then drew pictures for the remaining eleven words, including "have" and "is." Any picture that came to Lisa's mind was the right picture. For "have," Lisa drew a picture of two hands grasped together. For "is," she sketched our lunchroom table—go figure.

When Lisa came in from noon recess, we reviewed the twelve flash cards with their associated pictures. Lisa instantly looked at the word with its picture and said the word. Laying four cards in a line, I said, "Lisa, read this."

Without hesitation, Lisa read, "I have a dog."

I made a new sentence from four different cards and said, "Lisa, read these words."

She read, "His name is Sam."

While Lisa was "reading," Sarah came quietly down the stairs and tiptoed up behind Lisa as she read the third sentence: "I like Sam."

"Lisa," Sarah exclaimed, wrapping her up in a big hug, "You can read! How wonderful!"

Lisa's success indicated that a sight-word approach might work for her. Her success was due in part to her good visual memory, but it was the result of taking a novel approach that boosted her confidence, thereby removing her biggest barrier, self-doubt.

That evening, I reviewed an upcoming page from our book about tigers and wrote ten new words on a flashcard. The first thing in the morning, Lisa looked at the word while I said it. We did that for all ten new words. For the first trial through the flash cards, Lisa looked at each word. If she hesitated for even a moment, I said the word. On the third trial, she looked successively at each flashcard and said the word. Besides having a good visual memory, Lisa was able to use the story's context to identify unknown words. Her ability to use context was enhanced by having her first look at the pictures in the book and using the pictures to tell me what the story was probably about. The combination of these three skills—pictures, context, and sight words—was the ticket. Day after day, Lisa became a better reader,

A few weeks later, I introduced Lisa to a second-grade reader. We used the same approach of identifying ten new sight words, memorizing them, and then reading the passage from which the words had come. Following this strategy, we took turns reading short passages in the second-grade reader. From that point on, Lisa's acquisition of reading was simply a matter of practice.

When school got out that day, Sarah jauntily caught up to me in the parking lot. "Saturday" she said, "we will be making a long trip that will last several days. We need to get some things to take with us." Leading me to her car, Sarah opened the trunk of her war pony, as she called it and retrieved a hand axe and a ball of twine. She put them in the back of my pickup. "Let's drive down to the river," she said, pointing to the road in front of the school that, after few hundred yards ended up at a peninsula formed by a loop in the Tongue River. Dead ahead was a stand of young willow saplings. "We need twelve of 'em," she said.

We cut the saplings, trimmed away the branches for the first eight feet, and cut off their tips. Laying the saplings butt to tip, we bound them together with twine and put them in the back of the pickup. Next, we drove a half mile past the cemetery to where sagebrush grew in profusion. We cut and bound together four armfuls of sage. "We are ready," Sarah said with evident satisfaction. "We'll leave tomorrow morning and will be gone for five or six days. Bring the things you will need and don't forget our new tent."

CHAPTER SIXTEEN

Nowah'wus

*"When a great vision is needed, a man who has it must follow
the vision just as the eagle seeks the deepest blue sky."*

Crazy Horse, Oglala Sioux

Saturday, shortly after noon, I met Sarah at the school. She put several big tarps, a large bundle of old blankets, her usual traveling gear in the back of the pickup and hopped into the cab. At her direction, we took the Birney Road to its intersection with Highway 212 and turned east. In two eye blinks, Ashland was in the rearview mirror. Sarah rolled up her jean jacket and rested her head on it. Apparently, we were in for a long drive.

At Broadus, Highway 212 made a sharp right turn. A mile later, we crossed the Powder River Bridge and quickly came to a gravel road on our right that intersected the highway and paralleled the Powder River. Sarah gestured for me to take it. When we had gone about four miles, she pointed at a set of tire tracks that ended at the river. "Follow the tire tracks. It looks like they lead to the river. We'll camp there."

While Sarah was pulling supper out of her rucksack, I set up our new backpacker tent. Looking at it, Sarah said, "That will not do. You have the entrance to the lodge facing south. A Cheyenne lodge always faces east, toward the rising sun. We need to pull the tent pegs and rotate the tent."

After supper, we sat around our campfire while a gibbous moon made its way across the night sky. When it disappeared, we retired to our new tent. That night we educated the tent about carnal things. It was a thorough education. Afterwards, as we lay there in the darkness, Sarah mused, "I certainly am not a good traditional Cheyenne woman."

"What do you mean?"

"The traditional young Cheyenne woman was chaste because if she had sex before marriage, her family disowned her. If passion temporarily overruled good sense, as it sometimes does, she and her lover sneaked out of camp during the dead of night and went to live with the Lakota or the Arapaho. But if her lover would not take her away, the young woman found a stout tree and hanged herself."

"Why did she hang herself?"

"She had shamed her family."

Knowing how important it was for Sarah to follow the traditional ways of the Cheyenne, I became concerned about the implications of our licentious behavior. Yet Sarah's comments came lightly, with almost revolutionary zeal. "How do you feel about us having sex? Is it a bad thing?"

"It was a bad thing in the old days when we lived in small, close-knit groups. A loose woman would have put all the bulls in the village in rut. There would have been fights, and in some tepees the bonds of marriage would not have held. So, in the old days the Cheyenne tightly regulated people's behavior. But we no longer live in such close-knit groups. Times have changed. By the way, am I stealing you from a white woman who sleeps in a soft bed, wears expensive perfume, and is waiting for you to come back?"

"No!"

"Epeva'e. Then I don't have to hang myself, and we can do this often," she said, snuggling against me.

The sun was directly in your eyes when we reached Alzada, Montana — two trailer houses, a post office, and a bar with a gas pump. A half hour later, we came to Belle Fourche, South Dakota. A truckstop café called to my stomach, and I started to turn in.

"No! Not here," Sarah said, "This is a redneck town. Indians never stop here."

Three eye blinks brought us to the railroad tracks that bisected the town, and three more blinks put Belle Fourche behind us. The highway led south. Upon reaching the top of a ridge, we could see a town five miles farther south, at the base of the Black Hills.

Spearfish's business district was two blocks long. Many of the buildings were made of red sandstone, giving the town a picturesque touch. At the south edge of the town, we came to a junction. A right turn would have taken us up a canyon that a mountain stream had carved into the Black Hills. Instead, we headed east down a broad, U-shaped valley that ran along the north edge of the Black Hills.

"This is an unusual valley," I commented.

"What do you see that tells you this valley is unusual?"

"Notice the limestone outcropping along the edge of the Black Hills. It is bowed up, causing it to fit tightly against the base of the mountains. It's likely the limestone was left behind by the Cretaceous Sea, the same body of water that once covered the Northern Cheyenne Reservation. But here, something different happened. It appears that the Black Hills were thrust up and through the overlying burden of sedimentary rock. I wonder if this valley wraps all the way around the Black Hills?"

"It does. It's the racetrack."

"The racetrack? Did the Cheyenne once race horses here?"

"No, we didn't. It was a race between an exceptionally fast young man and a buffalo. All the animals took part on the buffalo's side. Well, all the animals except two. The magpie and the crow decided to be on the young man's team. All the runners made elaborate preparations for the race, painting themselves in the colors they wear today. When their preparations were complete, they gathered on the racetrack. At a signal, the race started. The swift birds shot forward like arrows. The jackrabbit, the deer, and the antelope were not far behind. But ahead of them was the young man and a few steps ahead of him was the buffalo. Have you ever seen a buffalo run?"

"No. I've never even seen a buffalo."

"You'd be surprised. Although buffalo are huge, they are amazing runners. A buffalo can be lying down and, if startled, can spring to its feet and in an instant be running at a full gallop. For a short distance, a buffalo can outrun a horse. If the race is long, a buffalo goes into a rocking lope and his tongue sticks out. Looking at that long tongue hanging out of its mouth, you'd think the buffalo is getting tired and will slow down. But the tongue is not sticking out because the buffalo is tired. Rather, the tongue is sticking out so the buffalo can suck more air into his lungs and get more oxygen to power his muscles. When a buffalo sticks out his tongue, he has just begun to run. If the race is longer than a mile, the buffalo will again catch the horse and then outrun it. The race that I am telling you about was long ago. It was a race all around the perimeter of the Black Hills, some three hundred miles. It was not just a race of speed. It was a race of endurance. No mammal, not the jackrabbit, the deer, or even the fleet-footed antelope, could keep up with the buffalo. As the runners neared the finish, the buffalo was well ahead of all the animals, even the young man. Everyone thought the buffalo was going to win. But the magpie had been flying high up in the air where he was out of sight and forgotten by everyone, including the buffalo. Just as the buffalo neared the finish line, the magpie shot down. He picked up speed in his dive, swooped ahead of the buffalo, and won the race. That meant the young man had also won because he and the magpie were on the same team!"

"Why were they racing?"

"Before the race started, the animals and the humans agreed that if the buffalo won, the buffalo would be above all animals, including man. It was also agreed that if the buffalo lost, it and the other animals would supply their hides and meat to sustain the needs of man. Because the magpie won, the Cheyenne gained the right to hunt buffalo and other animals. From that time on, the Cheyenne have hunted all animals except the magpie and the crow. To this day, the magpie and the crow are the Cheyenne's friends."

As Sarah concluded her story, we entered Sturgis. Reaching the middle of town, we came to a junction. "Go straight," she instructed.

As we rounded a curve and emerged out of a mountain valley onto the plains, Sarah pointed her arm northeast toward a tall, isolated mountain and exclaimed, "There's Nowah'wus!"

Nowah'wus (sometimes spelled Noahavose) is a huge, dome-shaped, nearly denuded mountain that rises majestically above the prairie, but it is not part of the Black Hills. Nowah'wus is a lava intrusion—a laccolite—that forced its way through the earth's crust sixty-six million years ago. The north and west side of the mountain bear the brunt of the winter winds that stifle the growth of vegetation and expose a rust-colored talus slope. At the top of the mountain there is a sprinkling of stunted pine. The east and south sides, being sheltered from winter's northwest winds, host a scattering of pine trees that grow thicker, straighter, and taller as the mountain plunges down to meet the prairie. At the base of Nowah'wus, the conifers mix with a few deciduous trees, which, in turn, give way to prairie grass.

Leaving the highway, we took a dirt road across a pasture and came to a gate. A sign on the gate read: National Park Service. That Nowah'wus is in the hands of the National Park Service is a good thing. It ensures that the spiritual and cultural home of the Cheyenne will be kept out of the hands of developers. After we crossed the cattle guard, the road made a large, reversed S and ended on a grassy slope a quarter of a mile from the base of the mountain. Looking south, it was surprising to see how high we had climbed above the plains in such a short distance. A light breeze whispered down from Nowah'wus, bringing us the scent of pine intertwined with the fragrance of the prairie. On that pleasant October day, Nowah'wus looked exactly as it appeared to the first Cheyenne who camped at its base roughly two hundred years earlier.

"The Lakota call it Mato Paha," Sarah said, "which Whitemen translate as Bear Butte, so named because when viewed from a distance to the south or to the north, the mountain looks like a lying-down bear. The Cheyenne call it Nowah'wus—the Hill Where the People are Taught. It's our Sacred Mountain, the center of our spiritual world. It is here that we come to gain favor with Maiyum, the spirit who controls the affairs of men. Maiyum brings us good fortune or bad luck. I have come here for my wu-wum, or as you might say, starving. If I am worthy, Maiyum will speak to me."

"Starving?" I exclaimed.

But Sarah did not hear me. She was unloading the willow saplings, bundles of sage, tarps, and old blankets from the back of the pickup. She laid the bundle of saplings on the ground and tied everything to them. Putting her rucksack on her back, Sarah picked up one end of the willow saplings and gestured for me to pick up the other. With her leading, we headed upward, toward the base of Nowah'wus. Before reaching the sharply defined base of the mountain, she turned to her right and started downhill, having navigated us around a ravine that started near the base of the mountain and ran southwest, deepening as it went. Three miles in the distance, the ravine lost its distinction and ended as it began, a slight depression.

After continuing downhill for a hundred yards, we walked over a slight rise and came upon an elderly Indian man sitting on the ground beside a small tepee. "Epeva'e wonowha," Sarah called out to him. Hearing her, the man stood and raised his palm in greeting. As we approached, his face broke into a broad smile. "You have done well, Moksisi," he said, eyeing our load. Turning toward me, he softly said, "I'm Willis."

Willis was a slender man of medium height with a long, narrow face aged by decades of wind, sun, and no doubt by years of contemplative observation. Clasping my right hand tightly in his, Willis placed his left hand on top of our joined hands and drew me close to him. Looking deeply into my eyes as if to view my soul, he said. "Thank you for bringing Sarah." Turning toward Sarah, he said, "Moksisi, today is a good day for a vision quest. Let's make ready." Willis led us to where he had cleared away the grass in an oval shape roughly six feet from east to west and four feet wide. He had dug a hole about a half-foot deep and two feet long in the center of the ellipse and had carefully piled and patted the dirt into a flat-topped mound eight inches high at the eastern edge of oval.

We set our load beside the oval, and Sarah unrolled the tarps and the blankets and untied the willow saplings. Willis distributed the saplings around the edge of the oval. Starting at the east end of the ellipse, he used a fist-sized rock to hammer a short, thick stick into the ground, and proceeded to make holes about every three feet around the perimeter of the oval-shaped space. He then stuck a willow sapling into each of the holes. That done, Willis grabbed the east-most sapling on the north side of the ellipse and bent it toward the middle. Sarah grabbed the eastmost sapling on the south side of the ellipse and did the same. Where the saplings met and for a short distance overlapped, Willis bound them together with twine.

With Sarah working on one side of the oval and Willis working on the other, the two of them bent over pairs of opposing willows and tied them together. Willis laid the two remaining willows from east to west over the dome, giving the structure additional strength. The oval-shaped frame was roughly four feet high in the middle.

Turning to me, Willis said, "Help me cover the frame with tarp." When the frame was covered with tarp, we layered old blankets over the tarp and put another tarp over them. Where the outer tarp touched the ground, Willis covered the bottom of it with dirt to prevent even a wisp of wind from sneaking into what I took to be a sweat lodge.

Willis then went to his small tepee and came back with a buffalo skull and a bundle of sage. The bleached-white skull had a streak of black paint running down its center. The eye sockets were painted red, and the skull's nose was stuffed with grass. Willis covered the mound of dirt in front of the sweat lodge with sage and carefully set the buffalo skull on it, positioning the buffalo skull so its eyes looked directly at the east-facing entrance to the lodge. Sarah took four bundles of sage inside the lodge, presumably covering the ground on the inside of the sweat lodge with the aromatic sprigs.

Willis made a second trip to his tepee and returned with a pail that contained fire-shattered stones. He sprinkled the stones on the ground to form a path from the buffalo skull to the entrance of the lodge. While sprinkling the stones, Willis took great care never to pass between the buffalo skull and the lodge. He then pointed toward a ridge line about a hundred yards to the northeast and asked me to go there and bring back twelve plate-sized rocks but cautioned me to never pass between him and the buffalo skull.

While Sarah collected wood, I carried rocks and put them in a pile. Willis took the wood Sarah had collected and leaned it against the rocks. He then gathered twigs and dry grass and placed them next to the wood. Striking a match, he set the tender on fire; it quickly crawled up the pieces of wood, heating the rocks.

Grabbing his pail, Willis announced that he was going for water and headed for the ravine, forty yards to the west. It was some time before he returned. When he did, Willis walked up to the sweat lodge, looked into an empty pail, and grunted "Humph," as if surprised. He went back to the ravine for water. Again, he was gone for a longer time than seemed necessary. When Willis returned, he looked in the pail, saw it was empty, said "Humph," and headed back to the ravine. He did this two more times. On the fourth try, Willis came back with water in his pail. He then whispered something to Sarah.

"Willis wants you to go sit on that rock," Sarah said, pointing to a big boulder about two hundred yards up the slope, "and be a wolf."

"Be a wolf?"

"Yes. Watch over the countryside. If you see anyone coming, go to them and tell them that the Cheyenne are praying to Maiyum. Kindly ask them to not disturb us."

Upon reaching the large boulder, I scanned the countryside and saw no one. When I looked down at the sweat lodge to give them an 'all clear,' my eyes were not prepared for what they saw. Sarah was clad in only her underpants and bra. Holding Sarah's clothes on his left arm, Willis reached down and opened the flap to the sweat lodge. Sarah got down on her hands and knees and, in an undignified manner, crawled inside. She reached out a hand to Willis, and he passed her the bucket of water and a foot-long, forked stick. Willis walked to his tepee and came back with a five-foot-long forked stick. He used the forked stick to secure hot rocks and slide them through the entrance of the sweat lodge. When all the hot stones had been passed into the lodge, Willis shut the flap and walked down the slope to his tepee. He returned carrying a long-stemmed ceremonial pipe that looked a lot like the pipe Sarah had used at the medicine wheel. Willis put tobacco into the pipe, tamped it with his index finger, and lit it. He held the stem up toward the sky and took a puff. Then he held the stem down toward the earth and took another puff. He offered the pipe to the four cardinal directions and to the buffalo skull. When the ritual was finished, Willis pulled back the flap to the lodge and passed the pipe to Sarah. After a time, the pipe came back out of the lodge. Willis refilled it with tobacco, repeated the smoking ritual to heaven, the earth, etc., and again passed the pipe into the sweat lodge. In all, this happened four times. When Sarah handed Willis the pipe for the fourth and last time, she crawled out of the lodge. He put a blanket around her.

Walking over to me, Sarah said, "Go to the pickup and wait for me. I won't be long." She and Willis then walked toward the tepee. I wondered why. Was it for more instruction?

After about fifteen minutes, Sarah came back to the pickup. She was dressed in her usual attire: hiking boots, jeans, and a long-sleeved shirt. "Let's go," she said.

"Go where?"

"To the top of Nowah'wus."

Looking up at the mountain, it seemed the hike would be arduous. It wasn't. A well-worn path started on the south side of Nowah'wus and gradually worked its way eastward to a saddle where giant, granite boulders protruded from the ground. Here, the trail crossed to the north side of the mountain, where it gradually wound upward in long, looping switchbacks. Upon reaching the top, we had a panoramic view. Looking east, our eyes followed the Belle Fourche River as it meandered toward the Cheyenne River, fifty miles to the east. Looking north, we saw two buttes on the horizon. Pointing at the butte to the east, Sarah said, "That's Deer's Ear Butte." It was aptly named; the twin peaks looked like a mule deer's long ears. Pointing to the rock-capped prominence further west, Sarah said, "That one is Captive Butte."

"Captive Butte, how did it get that name?"

"A long time ago, a Miniconjou band of Lakota raided a Crow village. They captured many horses and some Crow women. When the war party reached the head of the Owl River, which is now called the Moreau, they were well into Lakota territory and far from the women's home, so they stopped guarding their captives. That night, one of the Crow women escaped. In the morning, the Miniconjou searched for her. They searched for two days but could not find her. Concluding the Crow woman had made good on her escape, they struck camp. As they were riding away, one man looked back and saw the woman sitting in plain sight on the edge of the rock-capped butte. They were surprised that she had made herself conspicuous because when they recaptured her, she still had food."

Looking toward the south, we saw the Black Hills. Four mountain peaks defined its backbone. Gesturing toward the peaks, I asked, "Do they have names?"

"I don't know their Cheyenne names. I only know their ugly names."

"Ugly names?"

"The peak far to the south," she instructed, pointing her arm down the length of the Black Hills, "is Harney Peak. In 1855, General Harney ordered his troops to attack a band of Brulé peaceably encamped along the Platte River. The soldiers killed more than a hundred of them, including many women and children. Harney then marched through the heart of Lakota country, getting close enough to the Black Hills to see its highest peak. Being a man pumped full of self-importance, he named the tallest peak in the Black Hills after himself. The next one is Custer Peak. When Custer marched past it in 1874, he, too, named it for himself. The third one is Terry Peak. It is named for General Terry. He spent the summer of 1876 in the Yellowstone River Valley hunting Cheyenne and Lakota. The other peak, the one closest to us, is Crook Mountain, named for General Crook, the man whose soldiers attacked the Cheyenne and Lakota on Rosebud Creek just days before the Battle of the Little Bighorn. Isn't it something that the peaks of the Lakota's Pahá Sapa were named to honor Whitemen who found fame stealing our land and killing us?

As Sarah related the names of the four mountain peaks, a red-tailed hawk circled above us, looking for an unwary chipmunk, and two vultures rode the thermos along the side of the mountain on extended wings that never flapped. It seemed like we and the birds were the only living things in the world. But all too soon, Sarah said, "We need to go."

As we worked our way down Nowah'wus, Sarah paused four times to reach into her rucksack and retrieve a four-foot-long string to which was attached little balls of colored cloth—red, blue, or yellow. "Tobacco ties," she explained. "They are my offerings to Maiyum," Sarah explained as she hung a string of tobacco ties on to limb of a pine tree.

Two-thirds of the way down the mountain, we came to where

the trail passes by the granite pinnacles. "Go on without me," she said, "I'll stay here."

"What?"

"I am to stay here and wait for Maiyum to give me my vision."

"How long will you stay here?"

"I'll stay tonight, tomorrow night, and possibly as long as four nights. When Maiyum has talked to me, I will come down the mountain."

"Your rucksack looks to be empty. You don't even have a blanket. You can't stay up on this mountain, even for one night!"

"I'll be okay," she replied, "and don't worry. Ma'heo'o will look after me," Waving goodbye, she slipped off the trail and disappeared behind a large granite boulder.

Reluctantly, I headed down the mountain. With each step, my worry for Sarah increased. By the time I reached the trailhead, I needed assurance that Sarah would be okay alone on the mountain, and I went to find Willis. He was gone. So were the sweat lodge and his tepee. The only evidence that we had been there was the oval-shaped patch of bare ground and a string of yellow tobacco ties draped on the branches of a nearby ash tree.

That night, a cold wind swept down the mountain. Feeling it, I scanned Nowah'wus for the glint of a campfire that would assure me Sarah was not freezing to death. I could not find a reassuring glow.

Time is hard to kill when you are waiting for something to happen that does not adhere to the dictates of a chronometer. Each morning, just before sunrise, I brewed coffee on the chance Sarah would come down the mountain at first light. When she did not appear, I scanned the mountain to see if I could detect anything that might reveal her presence but never saw anything that gave me reassurance. I repeated the routine on day three. But by noon, my impatience got the best of me. I drove into Sturgis to fill the pickup with gas and to buy readily digested, quick-energy food to have for Sarah when she came down from the mountain. While there, a book in a store window caught my eye. It was *Old Yeller*, a book about a dog. Thinking that Lisa might find the story about a dog interesting, I bought it.

Wednesday morning, the sun had gotten a good start on its daily march across the sky before it woke me. Alarmed at having overslept, I sprang out of my tent, hastily put on a pot of coffee, and searched the mountain for Sarah. Seeing her coming down the last switchback, I ran to her. Even from a distance, she looked frightful. Her face was ashen. Seeing me, Sarah tried to run but her legs could not keep up with her body, and she fell. Luckily, the limb of a pine tree arrested her fall. Reaching her, I put one of her arms around my shoulder and practically carried her the rest of the way down the mountain. I propped her against the wheel of the pickup. Holding her chin in the palm of my hand, I put a cup of warm coffee laced with sugar to her lips. When she didn't respond, I gently pried open her jaw and poured a thimbleful of coffee into her mouth. It dribbled out. I tilted her head back and put in another thimble of coffee. Her Adam's apple moved, indicating she had swallowed it. I repeated this until a third of the cup of coffee had reached her stomach.

"Are you cold?" I asked.

She didn't answer. Sliding my hand under her shirt, I felt her stomach. She was hypothermic. Picking her up, I put her in the pickup, started it, and turned the heater on full blast as I frantically rubbed her limbs to induce blood circulation.

"More," she said weakly. Following the path of her eyes, I saw the coffee cup on the dashboard. As soon as it was placed in her hands, she took several swallows and then whispered, "Take me home."

We drove for two hours before Sarah said anything, and then it was but two words: "I'm hungry." I handed her a bottle of orange juice and a Hershey's chocolate bar. When we reached the Powder River breaks, Sarah pointed at the dirt road we had taken five days earlier. We did not go far when she gestured to a set of tire tracks that stopped at the edge of the river breaks. Below us, the Powder River meandered north through the ancestral land of the Northern Cheyenne. "It's beautiful, isn't it," she commented. Then, a tear came to her eye. It was followed by another tear and then another until a rivulet of tears flowed down her face. Putting a finger on her cheek and feeling moisture, Sarah realized she was crying, and she broke into chest-racking sobs punctuated by gasps for air.

When Sarah collected herself, she whispered, "Maiyum did not visit me the first night. By the second day, I was hungry. By the third day, I was famished. Even though it was the middle of the day, I was cold. I looked and listened for Maiyum, but I saw only the red-tailed hawk and heard only a blue jay. Just before daybreak of the fourth night, Maiyum visited me, and I had my vision. In my vision, I saw Ma'xeho'koneese'he, the hard-faced moon [The December full moon]. It rose in the east and slowly made its way across the night sky. It no sooner set than another hard-faced moon rose. As a succession of hard-faced moons made their way across the sky, I saw pictures, one after another. I readily understood the meaning of some of them, like the one of Joe placing Maggie's body on a limestone outcropping and, just as Maggie wants, building a rock coffin around her. But I could not understand the meaning of most the pictures. However, Maiyum promised me that when the time comes, I will understand what I saw. Ah," she said, laughing, "One picture was of myself many years from now. My hair was no longer shiny black. It had wisps of gray. I think that before I die, my hair will be mostly gray. I won't like that!

"Then the sun rose, and I started down the mountain. I felt warm, warm for the first time in days. I played and replayed my vision in my mind. I remembered that in my first hard-faced moon there was a picture of a man. He stood in the background, but he was supportive, understanding, and kind. He never laughed at my crazy ideas but listened patiently, and he always tolerated me no matter how hardheaded I sometimes can become. But in the moons that followed, that man was no longer there. I wondered why. So, I sat down on the trail and called out, 'Maiyum, come back! I have a question.'

"I waited and waited, but Maiyum did not come. And so, I called out again to him. But again, Maiyum did not come. I told the spirits that I was not going to leave their mountain until Maiyum came to me. I had a question he must answer.

"A breeze came down the mountain. Riding on it was Mistai, an owl. Mistai landed on a branch of a nearby dead tree. and he spoke to me. This is what he said. He said, 'Maiyum has given you your vision. It is a good vision. Why do you now call out for him?' 'Oh, Mistai,' I said, 'Thank you for coming. This is what I want to ask. In my first moon, there was a man. He was standing in the shadows, but he was there. Ask Maiyum why I didn't see him in any of my other moons.'

"Mistai flew up the mountain. When he came back, this is what he said. He said, 'You remember your vision as it was given to you,' and he flew away.

"I can't bear the thought of a life where you are not with me," Sarah said as she buried her head in my shoulder and sobbed anew. It did not seem like the time to debunk Native American mysticism, so I softly stroked her hair while she shed more tears.

In time, Sarah collected herself. "Is there a motel in Miles City?" she asked.

"Yes, there are several in Miles City."

"Then let's go there. I need a bath."

Good Riddance

"Be kind whenever possible, and it is always possible."

Dali Lama

When the sun came up Thursday morning, it found us barreling down the Tongue River Road, trying to get to school before the children arrived. Sarah's melancholy had been vanquished by a good supper, a hot bath, and a refreshing night's sleep. She was overflowing with enthusiasm. "I love this time of the year. The frost has killed the mosquitoes and sent the flies into hibernation. The mice, the chipmunks, the gophers, and the prairie dogs are scurrying about preparing for winter, and coyotes and badgers are busy hunting them. The deer, the antelope, and the elk are spending every waking minute eating so they will put on a layer of fat that will insulate them from the coming cold. The beaver are cutting willows, dragging them to the bottom of a deep pool and weighing them down with mud so they'll have food during the upcoming winter. The trees are adorned in their fall finery. It's all so beautiful. In the old days, the ten bands of the Northern Cheyenne came together in the fall to hunt buffalo. The buffalo hunt was a festive time. The young men preened themselves, vying for the attention of the attractive maidens. The older women visited with friends they had not seen in a year and catch up on the latest gossip. News was exchanged. Information was gathered. The men, serious in the hunt, were in their glory. The Council of Forty-four met to make tribal decisions. By tradition, the tribes of the Northern Plains did not make war on each other during the fall buffalo hunt. Still, it was best to be prepared. If the Nez Perce or the Shoshone ventured out of the mountains, the Blackfeet were likely to make it rough on them. And the Crow could never be trusted. Today, at this difficult time, the Northern Cheyenne need a buffalo hunt."

It was eight o'clock when we walked into the school. Maggie was in the kitchen. Sarah went to talk to her. Joe was in the boiler room, getting a fire going in the furnace.

"It's cold in here," he explained, striking a wood match against the side of the cast-iron boiler. "I want it to be warm for the kids when they get here. Old man winter is out there someplace. He'll show up any day now. Say," Joe said, looking as if he suddenly had a fantastic idea, "You have a gun, don't ya?"

"No, Joe, I don't have a gun. Why do you ask?"

"I thought that if ya saw old man winter sneakin' around, you could shoot him," he snickered, slapping himself on the thigh.

At that moment, the school's two vans arrived, and the children came running into the lunchroom like stormtroopers. Joe went to settle them down. After the children were ensconced in their classrooms, Lisa came down the stairs for her reading lesson.

"I have a surprise for you. It's a book called *Old Yeller*. We can read it together."

Old Yeller was set in the hill country of post-civil war Texas. It was about a dog that came to live with a frontier family. Although the story was set in the 1870s, the family lived much like the Indians live today on the Cheyenne Reservation. They drew their water from a well and took baths in the creek. They tended cattle, raised a garden, and lived off the land. While *Old Yeller* was more interesting to read than *See Spot Run*, it had some problems. For starters, there were too many big words for a beginning reader. But that was solvable. The main difficulty was passages like: 'Pa killed a Comanche who was trying to steal our mule,' and 'The family had to be vigilant so that bloodthirsty Indians didn't lift their scalps.' Racism, it seems, shows up in the most unexpected places, even in children's literature. I skipped over those occasional pronouncements.

Friday was ushered in by a cold, northwest wind that that hustled cirrus clouds across the sky and stripped the leaves off the deciduous trees, leaving them in threadbare garb. The Tongue River's denizens, human and otherwise, spent nearly every free minute preparing for winter. That morning, I set up my ladder on the south side of the school and began to caulk windows. When I met Joe for lunch, he said, "You have been busier caulkin' windows than a cow's tail at fly time. How many more windows do ya got to go?"

"Only the windows on the south side are left, and I've gotten a good start on them."

"I'm wonderin' if we have enough caulk to finish the job. Let's go look on the shelf and see."

There were eight tubes of caulk left. That set us calculating. How many windows had already been caulked? How many tubes had been used, and how many windowpanes still needed work? While we sat at a lunchroom table making our calculations, the children were outside for their after-lunch recess, Mrs. Johnson, the school's self-appointed rule enforcer, was supervising. Recess had not gone long when we heard a commotion outside. Looking up, we saw Mrs. Johnson coming through the basement door with Carol Standing Crow in tow. "Now put your nose up against the wall and stand there until you learn how to play nice. And don't move until I give you permission." With that, Mrs. Johnson went outside to resume her supervisory duties.

When recess was over, the children came in and went up the stairs to their respective classrooms. As they filed by Carol Standing Crow, she joined them. It was not long before the stairs reverberated with the sound of heavy clumps. It was Mrs. Johnson. She had Carol Standing Crow by the arm and was dragging the little girl across the lunchroom floor. Reaching the east-facing wall, Mrs. Johnson admonished, "I never gave you permission to take your nose off the wall. Now stand here until I say you can move. Do you understand me?" When Carol did not answer, Mrs. Johnson slapped her. "When I ask you a question, you answer me!"

Moving with the quickness of a mountain lioness protecting its cub, Maggie came out of the kitchen and pushed herself between

Mrs. Johnson and the little girl. Mrs. Johnson tried to push Mrs. Fighting Bear aside, but Maggie folded her arms across her chest and did not budge. As the two women stood toe to toe, glaring at each other, Sarah came flying down the stairs. Seeing Carol Standing Crow's tear-filled eyes, she picked up the girl and pressed the child to her shoulder. Mrs. Johnson erupted. "The little devil needs discipline, and you cuddle her! That's the problem at this school. These kids don't know the meaning of discipline. You spoil them!"

In a calm voice, Sarah said, "Mrs. Johnson, your work at this school is finished. It's finished for today. It's finished forever. You need to leave now."

"I'm not leaving!" Mrs. Johnson sneered. "And you can't fire me! You don't run this school. You're nothing but a squaw!"

Immediately, Joe was on one side of Mrs. Johnson and Maggie was on the other. As if they had choreographed it, they spun Mrs. Johnson around, and each grabbed one of her arms. They half-ushered and half-carried her out the basement door. Accepting the inevitable, Mrs. Johnson got into her car. As she drove away, the fired teacher rolled down her car window and shouted, "This is one Johnson you God-damn Indians aren't going to run out of the Tongue River Valley. I'll be back, and I'll have my lawyer with me."

After the school emptied that afternoon and everyone was gone, Sarah came down the stairs. "Let's drive out by the cemetery and go for a walk."

We walked along a logging road that paralleled Mission Creek and said everything that needed to be said through tightly clasped hands. Coming to a small, rounded knoll, we hiked up to it. From its vantage point, we looked down upon the little village that had grown up near the Birney Day School. Here and there, kerosene lanterns appeared in the windows of small, log cabins.

"What will Arneson say," I asked, "when Mrs. Johnson goes to him and demands her job back?"

"I phoned Arneson this afternoon and told him about the incident. He knows that Mrs. Johnson is a racist, and he has been waiting for an excuse to fire her. Now he has one. Mrs. Johnson is not coming back."

CHAPTER EIGHTEEN

The Substitute Teacher

*A lawyer will tell you that ownership is ninety percent
possession.*

As I neared the school Monday morning, a light-blue Chevrolet station wagon came down the Lame Deer Road slowly, as if searching for something. Seeing the school, the driver turned in and came to a stop in my usual parking spot. The door opened and out swung a pair of long, feminine legs. As the woman's toes stretched for the ground, she remembered something lying on the seat next to her. Leaning back to collect it, her pastel-yellow dress slid up, revealing a hint of sensuous thighs and delectable hips that curved back to a small waist. She had soft, rounded shoulders, the kind a man is instinctively drawn to put a protective arm around. Her flaxen-brown hair was drawn together at the nape of her neck and then cascaded down her back. But for the life of me, I can't remember the color of her eyes. However, I know they weren't blue. Blue wouldn't have fit, and what made this woman so stunningly beautiful was that everything fit, and it fit perfectly.

I intentionally parked so that she would have to walk by me to get to the school. As she approached, I introduced myself.

"Are you one of the teachers?" she asked.

"No. I'm the assistant janitor."

"Oh," she scoffed, walking dismissively past me.

When I stepped into the lunchroom, Joe immediately sought me out. "I have to leave for Billings this morning for training. They want to teach me how to do the job I've been doing here at the school for the past fifteen years. I'll be gone all week. So, it'll be up to you to keep the roof on this place. Every day, when it's coming up on recess, I want ya to get down off that ladder and sit it on the ground so that no kids come bursting around the corner and knock you and the ladder down. And don't get back on that ladder until recess is over and the kids are back in their classrooms." With that, Joe left for Billings.

When it was time for recess that morning, I did as Joe requested. I stopped caulking windows, laid the ladder against the foundation, and went to the lunchroom to scare up a cup of coffee. I had just sat down at a lunchroom table when I heard someone behind me ask, "My I join you?" Turning my head in the direction of the voice, I saw it was the new teacher. Without waiting for a reply, she sat down beside me.

As we drank coffee, "Annette" told me her story. She was born on the shore of the Pacific Ocean and raised in the morning shadow of the Continental Divide. She was doing her student teaching at Lame Deer when she was told to report to the Birney Day School because a first/second grade teacher was needed. Annette said that she would graduate in December and had a job waiting for her in Bozeman when the academic year resumed in January. "I'll be here until the end of the current semester, and then I'll go back to civilization and get on with my life." After a pause she said, "I've heard you're a doctor. Is that really true?

"I used to be."

"Oh. I see. You lost your license."

"No. I did not lose my license!"

"Well, what happened? Why aren't you a doctor now?"

"I got tired of it."

"You got tired of being a doctor and ended up on this God-forsaken Indian reservation working in this backwoods school as an assistant janitor? Pray tell, how did that happen?"

"It just happened, and I'm okay with it."

"But you won't be staying long, will you," she rhetorically commented. "Some weekend, you simply must check out Bozeman. It's an up-and-coming place. I'd be happy to show you around."

I don't know why, but I said, "I would look forward to it."

Perceiving my comment as an opening, Annette slid a little closer to me and became even more conversational, and maybe that was what I wanted. As we conversed, she got out her calendar and started running her index finger over the upcoming weekends. She was still searching her calendar when the children came in from recess. Annette followed her students up the stairs, and I waited for Lisa to come for her reading lesson.

When Lisa came into the lunchroom, she sat beside me and we took turns reading *Old Yeller*. We read that two range bulls fought in front of the family's house and would have caved in a wall had it not been for Old Yeller. Risking his life, the brave dog drove the ferocious bulls away. "Old Yeller sure comes in handy, doesn't he," I commented. Lisa nodded, but she had a forlorn look on her face.

"Is something wrong?"

"Not many pages left."

"You're right. We are almost at the end of the book. What should we do?"

Lisa shrugged her shoulders, but her eyes gave her away. She was looking at the bookshelves in the back of the lunchroom.

"Should we read other things in the morning and save *Old Yeller* for our last reading session of the day?" She nodded. Like two thieves conspiring to steal time, that is what we did.

The next morning, Annette again joined me for coffee in the lunchroom while the students were out for recess. She told me more about herself, relating that when she was six years old, her parents lived in Copenhagen. "I don't recall much about Copenhagen" she said, "But I remember the little mermaid sitting on a rock in the harbor. I want to go back and see the mermaid again and this time I want to see all of Denmark. Have you ever been there?

"No."

"You must go. You'd love it."

As Annette uttered that come-hither comment, the children came in from recess, abruptly ending out conversation.

For the rest of the week, Annette and I conversed over coffee at recess time, and I learned even more about her. Among other things, Annette told me that the most challenging part about preparing to be an elementary teacher was the required class in music. "I have many bones in my body," she mused, "but not one of them is musical. I was lucky the teacher liked me. He gifted me a B. If he had failed me, I wouldn't be here and I wouldn't have met you."

Late Friday afternoon, I was caulking windows when Sarah appeared out of nowhere. Standing at the base of my ladder, she looked up and said, "I could use your help!"

"Now?"

"Yes. Now!"

Sarah led me upstairs to her office. I waited for twenty minutes while she rummaged through shelves and file drawers, putting books in one box and documents, pamphlets, and letters into another. She finished sorting the materials just as school was over. Handing me one of the boxes and picking up the other, Sarah led the way out of her office. With a bob of her head, she motioned for me to accompany her as she walked into Annette's classroom.

"Annette," she cheerfully said, "it looks like the weather is going to hold for a few more days. Do you have plans for the weekend?"

"I'm going to leave immediately to drive back to Missoula to see my parents."

With the smile of the Cheshire cat, Sarah replied, "Johnathan and I usually go on an adventure every weekend, but not this one. This weekend, we are going to stay home and bring in our garden."

As soon as we were out of Annette's earshot, I said, "This is the first time that I heard we not only have a home, but we also have a garden! So, what was that all about?"

"You just got branded."

"Branded?"

"Branded, like a rancher brands his calf to let everyone know it is his. I just let that gold digger know you are branded and unavailable."

"Do you think that was necessary?"

"Definitely! Ever since she heard you're a doctor, she has been spinning her web around you."

CHAPTER NINETEEN

Bringing in the Garden

"When the last tree is cut down, the last fish has been caught,
Only then will you realize that you cannot eat money."

A Cree saying

Saturday morning, Sarah pulled into the school parking lot right on schedule. Rolling down her car window, she said, "Leave your outfit here and come with me."

Driving seven miles down the Birney Road brought us to a trail on our right. Sarah turned onto it. In a quarter of a mile, we came to a T-shaped log cabin sitting near the bank of the Tongue River. As we got out of Sarah's war pony, a black and white border collie greeted us. Wagging his tail, the dog went first to Sarah and then to me, searching for a hand that would pet him.

"Meet Ralph," Sarah said, "He's the Fighting Bears' official greeter."

Sarah knocked on the cabin door. No one answered. She knocked again, a little harder.

"Hold your horses, eh." Joe called out from inside the cabin.

We held our horses until Joe finally opened the door. Each hair on his head was marching to a different drummer, his shirt was unbuttoned, and his feet were bare. With a gesture, he invited us to come in and then retreated into his bedroom to finish getting dressed.

The cabin had three rooms. The largest room, the room in which we were sitting, was a combination kitchen/living room. A plywood counter ran the length of the north wall. There was a porcelain

126

sink without faucets in the middle of the counter. No faucets were needed because the cabin didn't have running water. Below the sink, the drain made a forty-five-degree bend, ran out the wall, sending any flushed water toward the river. Above the counter, wooden apple crates screwed into the wall served as cupboards. Where the cupboards ended at the northeast corner of the cabin, there was a propane-powered refrigerator. Halfway down the east wall was a door; it was the door behind which Joe had disappeared. A small table occupied the southeast corner of the room. It showcased the family's pictorial history. There was a picture of Joe and Maggie in their youth, holding hands and gazing doe-eyed at each other on their wedding day. Another picture was of a young man wearing a white shirt and a tie. "That's our son," Maggie explained. "He's off to Haskell getting his high school learnin' and doin' real good." The table also held a radio. Two wires ran out the back of the radio and down to a car battery sitting on the floor. There was an opening for second door in the middle of the south wall, but it did not have a door. Instead, an elk hide hung down over the opening that presumably led to a second, smaller bedroom. If the main room were elliptical, which it was not, the cabin's two main amenities occupied the foci. The north foci was occupied by a cook stove, the cabin's only source of heat. The big stove faced north, toward the kitchen counter and the cupboards, creating a kitchen area. A large, round oak table occupied the south foci. That was where we sat, waiting for Joe's Second Coming.

Eventually, Joe stumbled out of the bedroom and groped his way to the table. Maggie poured coffee into his cup. We patiently waited for the caffeine to work its magic on him. It took two cups to do the job. When it did, Joe's first words were, "Why's everybody sitting here like bumps on a log. There's work to be done. Let's get to it,"

The garden was located close to the river so that plants could sink their roots into life-sustaining, moist soil. It was guarded by a loosely strung woven-wire fence that seemed to be barely sufficient to stop a horse or a contented cow. A strand of chicken wire at the bottom of the fence kept out the rabbits and other rodents. Everything susceptible to frost had been picked. Only the root crops and acorn squash remained. Joe and I carried the squash to the root cellar behind the house. That done, Joe set me to pulling beets while he rubbed off their excess dirt and cut off their tops. He put the beets in one bucket and the tops in another. We hadn't worked long when Joe signaled it was time for a smoke. After taking a drag on his cigarette, he started the confab.

"Maggie and I usually get the garden in before this, but this year we got busy doing other stuff, and we are lucky because pretty soon big flakes of kimowan will start falling down out of the sky. I feel it in my bones that winter isn't too far to the north. What he said next was an unexpected shot across the bow. "And have your plans changed since the new teacher showed up?"

"Why would the new teacher affect my plans?"

"Well, she's some looker, and Maggie tells me that you and the new teacher have been comin' into the lunchroom every morning for coffee, and she sits right close to ya. It ain't me that's worried. It's Maggie. When Sarah's nouhkom was dying, Maggie promised her that she'd look after Sarah. What I'm saying is this. Maggie thinks Sarah has fallen so hard for ya cuz she's lonely. Maggie is worried that Sarah would take it hard if you were to get too close to that new teacher."

"Joe, I know it has been a little less than three months, but it is all the time I need. I am committed to Sarah. Don't confuse my being friendly with the new teacher and making her feel welcome at the school with me having romantic intentions toward her. But you said that Sarah is lonely. Why would she be lonely?"

"Sarah thinks she's been frozen out by many people on the rez, particularly the traditionalists. That ain't so, but it's what she thinks."

"Frozen out? Why would Sarah feel frozen out?"

"I don't know if Maggie wants me telling ya these things."

"This is between you and me, Joe. If I knew some of these things, I could do better by Sarah, as I promised you I would."

"Oui, I catch what ya mean. Well, there are two reasons. One of them happened long, long ago. Back in the eighteen nineties, Sarah's great-grandfather killed a man, a fellow Cheyenne. The man had it comin', but Sarah's great-grandfather should've taken the matter to

The Council of Forty-Four and let them say what should be done. But he didn't. Under Cheyenne law, he was pushed out of the tribe. He went from being someone the people respected and even honored to being a drunk.

"What was his name?"

"When a Cheyenne dies in dishonor, his name is never mentioned again. Most people have long ago forgotten about the killin', but not Sarah.

"You said that there are two reasons Sarah feels frozen out of the community. What's the other reason?"

"Sarah was gone from the reservation for a good while and came back just last spring. Once a Cheyenne leaves the rez, people is slow to accept 'em back."

"Why is that?"

"It because the people who left the rez saw things and did things no one on rez has ever done, and they resent what they call 'them smarty pants.'"

"Where did Sarah go?"

"That ain't my story to tell." Joe said, standing up. "We'd best get these beets up to the house. Maggie likely has water boiling and is ready for them."

Sure enough, Sarah and Maggie were ready to go into the canning business. A big kettle of water was boiling on the cook stove, and Sarah was putting canning jars into the water to sterilize them.

"We was thinkin' you two either died or went to sleep," Maggie said with a chuckle. Taking the pail of beets from Joe's hand, she continued, "And don't get comfortable! At the rate you two work, winter will be here before ya gets the carrots and the potatoes dug!"

The kitchen counter soon overflowing with vegetables that needed to be processed, but that was women's work. While Maggie and Sarah attended to it, Joe and I covered the windows with plastic and tacked new weather stripping around the door sill. By sundown, Maggie and Sarah had either canned the garden produce or put it in the root cellar, and Joe and I had put up a good defense against the coming cold weather. The Fighting Bears were ready for winter.

While lying on my cot that evening, I reflected on Joe's comment:

'Sarah was gone from the reservation for a good while and came back just last spring.' Where, I wondered, had she gone. I was dying to know, but since my previous attempts to learn about the path that brought Sarah into my life had only succeeded in putting emotional distance between us, I decided not to ask her. I was confident that when it became important for me to know that information, Sarah would tell me.

CHAPTER TWENTY

Crazy Woman Creek

What's in a name?
Sometimes more than we think.

The unseasonably warm weather continued all week, and everyone living in the Tongue River Valley regarded each of those days as a gift.

Monday, Sarah asked, "If I wanted to go someplace this next weekend, would you take me?" It was a rhetorical question. The only unknown was where we were going. Because she never answered such questions, it all boiled down to pragmatics: When do we leave and how long will we be gone?

When school dismissed Friday and the last child left for home, Sarah came bounding out of the school. She put her gear in the back of the pickup, and we were off. "Cross the bridge. At the junction take the Tongue River Road south," she directed.

That quickly brought us to and through White Birney. Reaching the Tongue River Reservoir, we drove past it and the nearby the post-office-town of Decker. Coming to Highway 87, Sarah gestured toward Sheridan. "Are you hungry?" she asked.

"Yes! Let's find a place to eat."

"No need," she replied, pulling two pieces of roast beef, two baked potatoes, and two bottles of Coke out of her rucksack.

Following Highway 87 south, we reached Buffalo, Wyoming. The little town was rolled up for the night. Turning a corner, my pickup's lights illuminated a small motel with a neon sign in the window flashing VACANCY. To one who lives in a tent, the promise of a soft bed and a hot bath was appealing. I touched the brake.

"Keep going," Sarah directed.

Twelve miles out of Buffalo, the headlights caught the name of a creek we were about to pass over: NORTH FK, CRAZY WOMAN CRK. It seemed the creek might have been named for a woman who had struggled mightily to feed, clothe, and keep house for her homesteading husband and their kids while living in a sod house on Wyoming's wind-swept, Godforsaken plains. The long winters, the hot summers, the isolation, the grasshoppers, the loneliness, and the ceaseless wind took their toll on many women homesteaders. It certainly did on my grandmother.

The story passed down in my family was that when the grandparents were out on their ranch during the Dirty Thirties, a hot wind blew hard out of the west almost every day. When the wind got so strong that it stirred up so much dust that the western horizon became dark, my grandmother climbed into a big steamer trunk and closed the lid after her. She stayed in the trunk until the wind ceased. Upon emerging, she'd smile like she just gotten up from a nap. My cousins referred to her as Auntie Loony, but my dad maintained that crawling into the trunk gave his mother the temporary reprieve she needed to keep from going crazy. Nonetheless, the lack of rain, the hordes of grasshoppers, and the relentless wind eventually drove my grandparents off their ranch.

So, what infamous deed had this pioneer woman done to warrant the honor of having a creek named after her? It must have been something quite titillating because a few miles farther down the road we came to another piece of geology dedicated to her memory: MIDDLE FK CRAZY WOMAN CRK.

"Slow down," Sarah directed as we came to the bridge. On the other side of the bridge, a dirt road came in from the left. Pointing at it, Sarah said, "Turn." A mailbox nailed to a fence post suggested the dirt road led to an unseen ranch house somewhere out on the prairie. If there was a ranch house down that road, we never saw it because after driving a couple of hundred yards, Sarah pointed at a big cottonwood tree twenty yards off the road. "Pull up by the tree and stop."

As soon as I turned the engine off, Sarah rolled down the window and listened intently. Hearing only silence, she opened the pickup door and stepped into the night. Just then a car came up the highway from the south. Its lights illuminated the top of the cottonwood tree and left us and the pickup in darkness. "Epeva'e," Sarah whispered. "Get our tent and your bedroll and follow me."

We walked to the creek. Following it downstream, we soon came to a little shelf of land between the creek and a cut bank. "Pitch the tent here," she whispered.

Once ensconced in our tent, my thoughts again turned to the creek's unusual name. "The highway sign calls this Crazy Woman Creek. How do you think the creek got that name?"

"It's named for relatives of mine."

"Seriously?"

"Seriously," she affirmed, rolling up her jean jacket to make a pillow.

"And?"

"And what?"

"And how did this creek come to be named for your relatives?"

"Oh, I see. You want to be told a bedtime story."

"Make it a lullaby."

"Can't do that."

"Why not?"

"It's a scary story."

"Okay. Tell me a scary story."

"Well, if you insist. I can tell you this story because it is night, so Maiyum will not be offended and cause me to wake up in the morning with a hunched back."

"Why would Maiyum inflict you with a hunched back?"

"Never mind. I cannot teach you all the Cheyenne ways in one night or maybe even in what remains of your lifetime. At any rate, a long time ago the men in a Northern Cheyenne village formed a war party intent on getting revenge on the Crow for their attack on their village the previous fall. The men left in early spring. They departed on foot because going on the warpath on foot brings the most honor. There are other reasons for going on the warpath on foot, reasons that probably must be explained to a Ve'ho'e, especially one from the East, like you. They went on foot because men on foot leave fewer tracks than men on horseback, and when danger is nearby a man on foot can easily hide and knows how to be quiet. A horse is hard to hide and understands nothing about being quiet.

"The men in the war party were gone a long time. As the days became weeks and the men did not return, the women started to worry. As the weeks turned to months, worry gave way to fear. When the months became a year, fear turned to despondency. The men had been gone too long. They surely had been discovered by the Crow and had been killed. They were never coming back. While no one in the village would say it aloud, in their hearts the women knew their husbands were dead. It was then the month of ripe chokecherries—August. More than a year had passed since the men had left on the warpath. While waiting for the men to return, The People had camped a long time in the same place. They had gathered all the firewood for miles, and their horses had eaten all the grass in the valley. The village had to move. Unable to accept that the men in the war party were never coming back, the women set out three piles of rocks in a straight line to show the direction the village had gone.

"When the village moved, they relocated on this creek, close to this very spot. Late one afternoon, four horsemen suddenly appeared in the north. When the horsemen realized they had been spotted, they immediately charged down on the camp, waving lances high over their heads. The women ran and hid while the old men prepared, as best they could, for battle. But the four horsemen were not Crow. They were Cheyenne. They were part of the war party that had left more than a year earlier. Crow scalps hung from the end of their lances.

"Singing songs of victory, the women prepared to welcome the main party, which they knew was not far behind. When the men of the war party came into the camp, they were dressed as they had been at the time of their fight with the Crow. They rode into camp side by side on fine horses. The warriors who had counted the most coup and who had captured the most horses rode in front. 'Here they come! Here they come!' the women shouted.

"According to tradition, the men's return with captured horses and enemy scalps called for the Victory Ceremony. It is the women's job to prepare for the ceremony, four days of feasting and dancing. Nothing, absolutely nothing, can be done until the Victory Ceremony has taken place. But that day, the women did not attend to their prescribed duties of honoring the warriors. Instead, when the men rode into camp the women pulled them from their horses and dragged them off into the bushes. In the bushes, the women did things with the men that cannot be talked about when children are present. Since then, the Cheyenne have called this stream The Creek Where the Women Went Crazy."

"That's quite a story!"

"Yes. But there is something else about the story that you should know."

"What would that be?"

"You should know that Cheyenne stories get handed down from generation to generation. As the stories are told and retold, the truth sometimes gets lost. When it does, the story becomes a cultural myth. The story about how Crazy Woman Creek got its name might be one of those cultural myths. It might not be true."

That night, I slept on the bank of Crazy Woman Creek. Beside me was a Northern Cheyenne woman. Based solely on personal experience, if the story about how Crazy Woman Creek got its name isn't true, it should be.

CHAPTER TWENTY-ONE

The Beginning of the End

*They are not dead who live in the hearts
of those they leave behind.*

The world was more shadow than light when a voice disturbed my sleep. "Get up or Ese'he will find you sleeping."
"That would be perfectly fine with me," I yawned.
"While you wake up, I'm going to take a bath."
"Where do you propose taking a bath?" I groggily asked.
"In the creek. Where else?"
The incredulity of the remark snapped my eyes open. "That water is straight from the mountains. It's only one degree warmer than an ice cube. You'll freeze!" My admonition went unheeded.

Later, as we reached the highway, the celestial artist was painting vertical streaks of pink-colored light across the eastern horizon. Fishing in her rucksack, Sarah found some venison jerky. Handing me a piece, she said, "Have breakfast."

We soon came upon Kaycee, Wyoming, a little town that anchored itself, as best it could, against the winds that swept down from the Bighorn Mountains. At the outskirts of town, Sarah gestured for me to turn west onto a gravel road. We went but a mile and then turned left onto a road that paralleled the Middle Fork of the Powder River. Ahead the Bighorns jutted up in front of us. I observed that the road did not climb the towering mountains. Clearly, we were nearing our destination.

"Have you been here before?" I asked.
"No."
"Do you know the way?"

"Have ye no faith?"

A few miles later, we came to where water gushed out of a small cut in a hill. As we crossed the bridge, Sarah announced, "That's the Red Fork of the Powder River. We're almost there."

A mile past the bridge, a dirt road came in from our right. Sarah gestured to take it. The road, if it could be called that, led us north up a valley. In two miles we came upon a dozen chickens dusting themselves in the dirt road. As the pickup drew near, the chickens squawked and ran toward a set of old log buildings that served as a ranch headquarters. At that point, the road deteriorated into a trail; it led us to the Red Fork of the Powder River. On the other side of the river, a wall of blood-red limestone rose three hundred feet above the valley floor. Here, the trail forked. Sarah gestured toward the one on the left. It took us away from the river and appeared to be without a destination.

"Are you sure this is the right way?"

"Yes."

In a short distance, the trail led back to the Red Fork of the Powder River, where protruding rocks did their best to punch a hole in the oil pan. Soon, the tire tracks led into the river. I stopped.

"Why are you stopping?"

"You don't think we should try to cross that river, do you?"

"Definitely!"

"We'll get stuck!"

"We won't get stuck. It's autumn. The river is shallow, and it's running over rocks. Just go slow and we'll make it. After all, the pickup is a Ford."

Once across the river, we followed the trail. After three rock-strewn miles, the trail started up a mountain that only a jeep could climb. To our immediate left, the Red Fork River came frothing white and angry out of a narrow gorge. "We'll walk from here," Sarah announced, pointing toward a gorge through which the Red Fork of the Powder River flowed. The farther we walked up the gorge the higher the sides rose above us. Soon, the gorge was so narrow and its walls were so high that we could see only a thin slice of blue sky above us. Sarah scrambled over rocks and boulders with an intensity that announced she was on a mission. After three miles of rock scrambling, we came to where the gorge opened onto a beautiful, oval-shaped, mile-long meadow that began at the base of the Bighorns where two streams came leaping down the side of the mountain and crashed together in a jettison of white spray to form the Red Fork of the Powder River. When the stream reached a gently contoured meadow, it quieted.

The meadow was surrounded by steep-sided terrain. To the north, a mountain with a base of bare sandstone jutted out from the Bighorns. Higher up, pine trees wrapped the mountain in a horizontal ribbon of dark green. The top of the mountain was crowned with a recent dusting of white snow that sparkled in the clear mountain air. At the west end of the meadow, a ranch was tucked snugly up against the mountains. Between us and the ranch buildings were three rows of abandoned pickups, caterpillars, sheep wagons, horse trailers, and horse-drawn buggies—every man-made mode of transportation the West had ever seen. The south side of the amphitheater was formed by a wall of red sandstone. Although the south wall rose only seventy feet, it would have been impenetrable were it not for a road coming from the south that a D-9 caterpillar had carved to the ranch headquarters.

While I was taking in the setting, Sarah struck out for the gradually rising, south side of the meadow. Partway up the incline, she sat down beside a dry irrigation ditch that paralleled the river. When I reached her, she said, "Smell the death."

I took a deep whiff but smelled only the fragrance of pine trees brought down the mountain by a light breeze. However, the faraway look in Sarah's eye suggested the death she smelled was in the long ago. Sweeping her arm down the length of the meadow, she said, "This was the beginning of the end."

"The end of what?"

"My culture, the traditional culture of the Northern Cheyenne. It died here! After we killed Custer in the summer of 1876, Morning Star moved our band here thinking the U.S. Army would never find us in this hidden valley. But just as the sun was rising on the morning of November 25, 1876, soldiers burst out of that gorge," she said, gesturing toward the gorge we had just traversed. "They attacked Morning Star's village. The women and children ran out of their lodges and into the mountains. The fighting lasted all day. Three of Morning Star's sons were killed. He was wounded five times, but they could not kill him because his medicine was too powerful. The Cheyenne warriors were forced to retreat into the Bighorns, enabling the soldiers to take over our village. The soldiers built bonfires and threw in everything that could not be carried away. They burned our winter supply of dried buffalo meat and our tepees, some of which had irreplaceable paintings on the inside that told our history. The soldiers burned hundreds of our buffalo robes, beautiful quilled and beaded clothing, hide shields, and moccasins. They even burned the last two ears of our sacred corn. Anything that could not be consumed by fire was broken. When the soldiers were done, every iron kettle had a bullet hole in the bottom.

"In the darkness of night, the survivors moved farther into the safety of the mountains. Most of them had only the clothes they were wearing, and some had fled from their lodges only partially clad. A few didn't even have moccasins. That night, the temperature fell to twenty below zero and a blizzard set in. The blizzard lasted two days and left snow two feet deep. Horses were killed so little children could be kept from freezing to death by placing them inside the animals' warm rib cages. Still, eleven babies froze to death that night. The next day, the men went ahead to build fires every few miles so the women and children could warm themselves. Despite these efforts, three more infants died, and fourteen adults were badly frostbitten. The survivors traveled through the deep snow for days before descending to the prairie and going in search of help. On the eleventh day, emaciated and starving, they stumbled into Crazy Horse's camp, located where Beaver Creek flows into the Powder River. The Oglala war chief and his people took the survivors in and shared what little they had with them."

Sarah paused for a moment. After taking a deep breath, she angrily stabbed her finger at the meadow and yelled, "Damn him! Damn him! Damn him!"

"Damn who?"

"Damn Last Bull. He caused this!"

"What did Last Bull do?"

"We knew the soldiers were nearby because four Cheyenne

wolves had discovered General Crook's camp and had come into Morning Star's village to report that soldiers were not far away. Several headmen wanted to move the encampment up into the mountains and build breastworks for protection. But Last Bull would not allow it. His Kit Foxes had recently returned from a war expedition against the Shoshone. They had taken scalps. Disregarding the wolves' report that soldiers were close, Last Bull demanded that everyone in the village stay and hold a Victory Dance to honor his clan's young warriors. When some Cheyenne tried to leave, Last Bull directed his dog soldiers to cut the cinches on their saddles."

After a long moment of contemplative silence, Sarah continued her story. "For the Cheyenne, going on the warpath was more about courting than it was about killing. A young man went on the warpath so he could count coup, meaning touch an enemy, be the enemy dead or alive, and thereby prove himself worthy of a woman's attention. He went on the warpath to acquire the horses needed to convince a certain young woman's family that they should consent to the marriage. If no woman in his camp would allow the young man to pull her aside and wrap his blanket around her, he went on the warpath to capture a young woman of another tribe and bring the woman back to cook his meals, bear his children, and, in time, learn to love him. But when the U.S. Army marched into our land, war was no longer about life. It was about death."

Abruptly standing, Sarah struck out for the pickup with strides that were, even for her, unusually long. I followed slowly. When I got to the pickup, she was sitting in the cab, waiting. Her jaw was clinched tight. The veins in her neck were engorged with blood.

"Are you angry?" I rhetorically asked.

"No!" she snapped. "I'm not angry!

"You look pretty irate."

"Maybe I was earlier, but now I am sad. I am sad for my ancestors who died in that meadow. Many of them were young. I feel sad because they died without having children who would keep their memories alive. I am saddened by how the Cheyenne are forced to live today. You've seen it. The children look out at the world with vacant eyes that see no future.

When we reached the main road, Sarah audibly exhaled. With a softened voice, she said, "Once, a long time ago and before Whitemen came into our land, a prophet lived among us. His name was Sweet Medicine. Before he died, Sweet Medicine foretold the future, saying 'Strangers will appear among you. Their skins will be light colored, and their ways will be powerful. The buffalo will disappear, and another animal will take its place, an animal with slick hair and split hoofs. You will learn to eat its greasy flesh, and your ways will change. You will leave your sacred religion for something new. You will lose respect for your leaders, start quarreling with one another, and take up the fair skins' ways. You will become worse than crazy.' It is as Sweet Medicine foretold. We have lost our way."

CHAPTER TWENTY-TWO

Busby, Montana

"Poverty is not just a lack of money; it is not having the opportunity to fulfill one's potential as a human being."

Amartya Sen

There was no school Thursday or Friday so the teachers could, if they wanted, attend the Montana State Teachers' Conference in Helena. None of the teachers at the Birney Day School went because the drive was too far and the expenses were too great.

At ten o'clock Thursday morning, I met Sarah at the schoolhouse. Putting her rucksack, a long-handled shovel, and a gunny sack in the back of the pickup, she climbed into the cab and instructed, "Head toward White Birney."

At the outskirts of the village, we turned left onto the Hanging Woman Creek Road. As we topped the divide separating the Tongue River and Otter Creek, Sarah gestured for me to pull off the road. "Come," she said. Retrieving her shovel and the gunny sack from the back of the pickup, she slipped under the barbed-wire fence that paralleled the road. Upon reaching a patch of brown-husked plants that stood ten to twelve inches tall, she pointed to them and said, "In the summer, this brown husk is the foundation for a purple flower. We call them as they look, purple coneflowers." Digging up the plant's root, she handed it to me and said, "Put a piece of this root in your tea every morning and it will ward off the flu and colds, and you'll stay healthy this winter."

We scoured the hillside for purple coneflowers. The plants, having lost their flowers weeks before, were hard to find amidst the sagebrush. When we found a cluster of them, Sarah took only every tenth plant so that there would be an adequate number of coneflowers next spring. As we collected the roots, clouds looking like giant marshmallows slowly danced their way from west to east, ushering in another Montana-perfect, fall day. Yet, the calendar advised that Christmas was not far off.

"School lets out for Christmas, doesn't it?" I asked.

"It usually does."

"Over Christmas break, let's go to where there is an ocean whose water is warm and there are miles and miles of sandy beach."

"Look," she said, pointing at a platoon of ants carrying off a dead grasshopper. Squatting on my haunches, I pretended to show an interest in the ants, but my exasperation was too much to contain.

"Sarah, I just asked you whether you'd like to go somewhere warm and tropical over Christmas break. Are you interested?"

"Look at how the little ants work together to carry off that big grasshopper. That grasshopper weighs a hundred times more than any one ant. Isn't it amazing how much can be accomplished by working together?"

While still squatting to pretend to look at the damn, dead grasshopper, I exclaimed, "Sarah, why aren't you answering my question?"

She tackled me with the full force of her weight and sent me sprawling. With catlike quickness, she straddled me. Grabbing my hair, she banged my head against the ground. "Damn you! Damn you, Damn you!"

To keep from getting my brains bashed out, I grabbed her wrists and held them tightly. As tears streamed down her face, she pleaded, "Don't you see? Don't you understand? My people are poor. They are lost. Every day they drift farther from our Cheyenne ways, and I don't know how to help them. I don't even know if I am strong enough, capable enough, or worthy enough. What kind of person would I be if I let my rich boyfriend spirit me off to a far-away, exotic place during Christmas while my people struggle in twenty below weather to keep from freezing to death?"

Seeing contrition written on my face, she softened. "Saturday we'll go to Busby. Then you'll understand."

Saturday, I met Sarah at the school at two o'clock. I expected that she would, as usual, leave her car and ride with me to Busby. Instead, she wagged her finger at my pickup and said, "A Whiteman's shiny new pickup can't possibly sneak undetected into a Cheyenne village. We'll take my war pony. Put your things in the backseat."

Instead of heading west to Lame Deer and then on to Busby, the most direct route, Sarah drove east across the Tongue River bridge. "Aren't we going to Busby?" I asked.

"We're taking the great circle route," she replied. At the junction, she turned south onto the Tongue River Road. Evening was approaching when we reached the Tongue River Reservoir. There, at the mouth of the South Fork of Monument Creek, Sarah turned right. She drove a few hundred yards down the lightly graveled road and again turned right onto a tire-track that led up a barren valley. Upon reaching a clump of short, water-starved pine trees, she stopped. "We'll camp here," she announced.

The next morning, we broke camp and set out on the thirteen-mile loop that led to a north-south gravel road. There, she turned north, onto a road that took us down the valley of Rosebud Creek. Jack Frost had recently paid a visit, splashing the leaves of the deciduous trees with pleasing colors of light yellow, soft red, and here and there, a tinge of gold. Reaching Highway 212, we turned east and in a short distance came over a small rise. A mile ahead and around a sweeping left-hand curve was Busby, Montana.

The little town sat on a bone-dry hill like a vulture on the carcass of a month-old roadkill. A Standard Oil gas station hugged the south side of the highway. Adjacent to the filling station was a recently constructed building in the shape of a gargantuan wooden tepee, apparently erected with the expectation it would magnetically pull in the anticipated, culture-hungry tourists coming down the newly paved highway to see Custer's Last Stand, twenty-five miles to the west. That fantasy vanished before the last shingle was nailed down. Now, the wooden tepee was unkempt, uninviting, and unused. An Indian leaned up against it. He wore a torn sports coat, blue jeans, and right-out-of-the-box cowboy boots. Turning his head to watch us go past, I saw that his nose was splayed across his face and bleeding. "Should we stop and see if he needs attention?" Sarah kept driving.

"Do you know him?"

"His name is Fred. He just got back from a relocation program, the government's latest ploy to rid the reservations of Indians. They send Indian men off to a big city for a few weeks, give them money for a month or so, provide some vocational training, and then get them factory jobs. It never works. They soon come back to the reservation, worse for the experience. Dejected, defeated, and deflated, they grab a six-pack of beer and go straight to the blanket. Most of them eventually sober up, and, in one way or another, get on with their lives. Fred will do that when he's ready."

A little farther on, we came to a small, white-colored house on the north side of the highway. It served as the town's grocery store. Paper wrappers and empty boxes littered the ground around it for a hundred yards in every direction, advertising that the store sold milk, bread, sugar, candy bars, pop, chewing tobacco, and cigarettes—lots of them.

When we came to the post office, Sarah pulled into a parking spot. "Let's walk so you can get to know Busby." We walked north, down a serpentine, dirt road that wove its way past ready-to-fall-down, log cabins. Each cabin had an outhouse. Beside every residence there were one or two abandoned cars. Some of the cars had colored cloth draped over their windows, providing privacy for whomever had taken up occupancy. Even though it was a nice fall day, the only visible signs of life were dogs that skittishly approached us hoping we might throw them some food. The dogs were about fourteen inches tall and had surprisingly short hair, considering the coldness of the winters in Montana. They were so thin one could count their ribs. Their stature was consistent with Darwin's theory of evolution—those who survive are those best adapted to their environment. Because most of the reservation dogs appeared to be on their own, their survival depended on finding a scrap of food here and a nearly meatless bone there. The slim pickings in Busby favored small dogs.

Busby was not laid out in a grid. Instead, it evolved along paths that, in time, became dirt roads. We traversed two of these irregular blocks before the first person came into sight. It was an old woman shuffling toward the post office. The woman did not lift her eyes from the road as we passed, suggesting that she did not want to acknowledge our presence. Fifty yards farther, we saw an old man coming around the corner of his log cabin. When our eyes made contact, he turned in his tracks and disappeared behind his house. In front of the next place, two adolescents sat on the hood of an abandoned car and looked out at the world with expressionless eyes. I gave them a discreet wave. They didn't wave back.

We then came upon a graded street that ran true north and led to two well-maintained, two-story buildings, the school and its dormitory. Their government-precise appearance made the buildings look cold, sterile, and insultingly out of place. A newly made east-west street was to our west. There were four brand-new but unoccupied frame houses on the south side of the street and four houses on the north side. The eight houses were the exact copy of the other except for color. On the north side of the street, the first house was pastel yellow, the second was pastel blue, the third was pastel green, and the fourth house was pastel pink. The four houses on the other side of the street repeated the color scheme, but in the opposite sequence. Scars across the development indicated the houses had water and sewer. Freshly set utility poles waited for wires that would bring electricity. A 500-gallon propane tank behind each house predicted a furnace. "That looks like progress" I said, pointing at the new houses.

"Tract housing. It's the BIA's [Bureau of Indian Affairs] latest plan. They think that if they put us Indians in Whiteman houses, we'll become Whitemen. Well, it won't work. The Indian who walks into his new house tomorrow will still be an Indian five years from now."

"Sure, he'll still be an Indian, but he will be a better-off Indian. Living in houses with electricity and indoor plumbing has to be better than living in a run-down, log cabin with an outhouse."

"We've never had a government program that, in the long run, helped us. Why should things change?"

"That sounds a little cynical. And what do you mean, no government program has ever helped?"

"There was a time when our men hunted from the Yellowstone River to the Arkansas River to provide meat for the tribe and buffalo hides for our lodges. Life was good. In 1868, we signed a treaty, thinking it was a peace treaty. Little did we know that the treaty would allow a railroad to be built along the Platte River. The railroad brought white hunters who killed buffalo by the tens of thousands. We were told not to worry about the slaughter of the buffalo because the government would feed us. What did they feed us? They fed us wormy flour and rancid bacon, and barely enough of it to keep us from starving to death. Rations turned our culture on its head because it took away the Cheyenne men's pride of being the providers. Embarrassed, the men sent their wives to the ration house to stand in line like beggars to get the government's handouts. Busby started off as a ration station. For that matter, it still is. But now, the post office is the ration station."

"What do mean, the post office is the ration station?"

"It's where the welfare checks come. Most of the checks come to the unwed mothers. Because there are no jobs on the rez, having children is about the only way to earn a little money. As a result, nearly half of our population is under the age of eighteen. The babies born today will, in a few years, become bored teenagers. As the saying goes, idle hands are the devil's workshop. Alcoholism will become even more rampant, and the use of that new drug, LSD, probably will become the in-thing. That brings us to the government's next hollow promise. We were told to educate our children so they will have a way out of poverty. That is what we did and are still doing. Our children do as well in school as white kids until about the sixth grade. Then one day they learn the meaning of future, and the next day they realize they don't have one, and they give up. A high school education or even a college degree will not get you a job in Busby because there aren't any jobs to be had.

It seemed time to change to topic: "Where did the Cheyenne live before a ration station drew them into Busby?"

"When the first Northern Cheyenne came back in 1880, they

scattered themselves along Lame Deer Creek, Muddy Creek, and Rosebud Creek, and they lived in tepees. When the tepees wore out and there were no buffalo from which to make new coverings, they built log cabins. Every family raised a garden in the fertile creek bottoms. In late summer, they gathered wild fruit and dried it to eat during the long winter. Come fall, the men sawed wood, split it, and stacked it beside their cabins for when the snow came. They had things to do. Activity gave their lives purpose and meaning, and having meaning in one's life leads to contentment. But what is there nowadays to keep the people in Busby busy and content? No one who lives in a tract house will raise a garden because Busby sits on a gumbo-covered hilltop. No one who lives in Busby will dig a well; they'll just turn a faucet and water will come out. No one who lives in Busby will go into the hills to gather wood; they'll just click on the furnace. When the propane tanks go dry in the middle of the winter, the BIA will send someone to fill them so the water pipes in the government's tract houses don't freeze. No one who lives in Busby will get out of their house to talk to their neighbors and find out what is going on in their community. They'll just sit in their whiteman houses and listen on the radio to a Whiteman in Billings tell them what the weather is like on the other side of their front door. The BIA isn't building a town. It's creating a ghetto populated by jobless men, alcoholics, unmarried mothers, and kids with no future."

Our counterclockwise walk around Busby had come full circle, bringing us back to the post office and Sarah's car. As Sarah flicked the reins of her war pony, I said, "Thanks for showing me Busby. Seeing the town explains a lot. You're right. It's pretty much hopeless."

"I said we have problems. I never said it's hopeless. Hopeless happens only when you quit trying."

"Are you still trying?"

"As a matter of fact, I am. At least I am searching for answers."

"Have you found any?"

"Maybe. While on Nowah'wus, Maiyum told me that if the Northern Cheyenne are going to heal and survive, we must go back to our traditions. He showed me pictures to give me guidance as to how that can be done. But there are many pictures whose meaning I do not yet understand, and that has me tossing and turning many nights. Last week, I dreamed about the picture Maiyum had shown me of a white woman reading to her young child from a book. The book had a picture of a buffalo and a magpie on the cover. In my dream, I turned the pages and saw that the book told the story about when our best runner and a buffalo raced to determine who was fastest over a long distance. Then it came to me! I realized that we should make children's books. We can do that! Our elders know a great many stories traditionally told to our children. In some families, the stories are still told. Each story has a purpose. Some stories tell about our origins, and others tell who we are. Many of our stories teach children values, such as the shortcomings of being dishonest, the importance of being brave, how to be compassionate, or why one should share with the needy. Often the story is told through the eyes of an animal. They are wonderful stories."

"How would you go about getting the stories made into books?"

"I asked myself that very question. Then, just a few nights ago, the answer came to me, again in a dream. I dreamed about a big gathering of our elders, the keepers of our stories. In my dream, I saw young people listening while the elders told stories. The young people wrote down what they heard.

"The dream meant that we should have a big gathering of story tellers, writers, and artists. They will split into teams, each team will consist of a storyteller, one or two writers, and several artists. But we will need help. No one on the rez knows how to make a book, so we will have to look outside for that knowledge. The imported expert will circulate from team to team, giving suggestions, advice, and encouragement. Instead of sending the manuscripts in search of a publisher, we will print the books right here on the rez. Think about it, books for children that are illustrated, colorful, and tell a good story published by the Northern Cheyenne Press. Soon, royalties will be coming in for each member of a team that got a book published. Someone will be hired to market the books. Someone else will have the job of packaging the books and putting them in the mail. But more important than the money and the jobs they will generate is the pride it will give the Northern Cheyenne."

"That sounds like a good idea, an excellent one!"

"The idea might be good, but there is one huge problem."

"What's the problem?"

"No money. It will take money to get the book project up and running, and I have no idea where to find it."

"Sarah, there are people out there with deep pockets who would love to support the project you have in mind. You only have to determine how much money you need, scout out the potential donors, determine what about the project appeals to each donor, and be well prepared to make your case."

"Do you think it's that simple?"

"It's not simple. It might not even work, but it's worth trying."

"Do you want to hear about another picture I saw on Nowah'wus?"

"Sure."

"The picture was of a Cheyenne elder standing on Little Bighorn Battlefield and talking to a group of white people. The tourists were listening intently as the elder told them about the battle. I asked Maggie what she thought the picture might mean, and she said it means our elders should give tourists guided tours of nearby historical sites. Think about it. Would you rather be at the Little Bighorn Battlefield listening to a twenty-something kid from New Jersey tell you what he learned about the battle from a history book, or would you prefer to listen to a Cheyenne elder share with you what happened there? Our oral tradition is strong. The Cheyenne elder would be able to point to a spot and say, 'That is where Bearded Man, a valiant warrior, died.' Moving farther along the hillside, the elder would come to a spot and say, 'This is where Lame White Man, my great-grandfather, died. He was killed in an unfortunate mistake.' The elder would then tell the visitors about the mistake that resulted in Lame White Man's death.

"We have more to show our visitors than the Custer battlefield. There is the Powder River Battle. It occurred in March 1876 and was the beginning of the army's campaign to force us and the Sioux onto reservations. That battle took place forty miles southeast of White Birney. There is the Rosebud Battlefield where the Northern Cheyenne led by Two Moon and Spotted Bear fought General

Crook and over a thousand of his soldiers for eight hours before driving them off. But we do not call it the Rosebud Battle. We call it the battle where the sister saved her brother. We would also show our visitors where the Battle of Bear Mountain took place in January 1877. It was there that Colonel Miles and five hundred soldiers attacked a village of Indians, some were Crazy Horse's band and the others were Northern Cheyenne. The Battle of Little Muddy Creek, also called the Lame Deer Fight, occurred in the spring of 1877, not more than a mile and a half from where the town of Lame Deer is today. Our elders could guide our visitors to these sites and explain what occurred there. All we need is a van that will hold a couple dozen people. Of course, our visitors will have to be fed. That means jobs for several women who will prepare mid-day box-lunches and provide liquid refreshments.

"When this touring thing takes off, we will want to provide lodging for our guests. I don't mean single rooms in a cheap motel, but a nice lodge with a tall, stone fireplace and a common dining area with heavy, wooden tables where our guests will gather and get to know each other as they eat good food cooked by Cheyenne chefs. We will add to our visitors' experience by having elders come to the lodge in the evening to tell our guests more about the Cheyenne history, our culture, the plants we use for healing, and our traditions. The lodge will have a bookstore offering children books written by Cheyenne authors and illustrated by Cheyenne artists. We will also sell books about the Northern Cheyenne written by scholars such as Mari Sandoz, Father Peter Powell, George Bird Grinnell, Paul Hedren, and our own John Stands In Timber. The lodge gift shop will sell only things made by our Cheyenne people, things like star quilts, women's dresses made of soft deer hides and decorated with porcupine quills and elk teeth. For the men, there will be leather vests and jackets, and chaps. The gift store will also sell artwork done by our people. One thing we will not sell is coffee mugs showing a picture of Two Moon or rubber tomahawks made in Japan. We will not stage phony Indian dances intended to provide entertainment or do anything that denigrates our culture.

"In time, the guided tours will become the foundation for the next venture. Every summer we will offer college courses on the history, culture, and traditions of the Northern Cheyenne to groups of fifteen to twenty college students who will receive instruction, visit the historic sites, and stay at our lodge. Because our history has too often been told by people whose skin is white, our tribal elders will provide the instruction. So, what do you think of my crazy ideas?"

"The ideas don't sound crazy to me. They sound like a dream too big to let die."

"Do you want to hear about one more picture I saw that night on Nowah'wus?"

"Definitely!"

"The picture was of a herd of buffalo. That was it, just a herd of buffalo. For the longest time I could not understand its meaning, but I kept dreaming about the buffalo night after night. It was not until I dreamt about that herd of buffalo for four consecutive nights that the meaning came to me."

"And?"

"The meaning is that we should find about fifty thousand acres on the rez and bring in buffalo. Stocking the buffalo pasture will not cost anything because there are more buffalo in Yellowstone Park than they know what to do with. Fencing our buffalo pasture will not cost much. Instead of putting in fence posts, we'll string strands of barbed wire from pine tree to pine tree around the perimeter of the buffalo pasture. When the herd grows, we will offer buffalo hunts to rich Whitemen. They will not be allowed to drive out into the pasture in a jeep and shoot their buffalo from the vehicle. Instead, they will have to hire a Cheyenne guide who will take them into the buffalo pasture by horseback or on foot. When they shoot a buffalo, the white hunters can either field-dress it and pack it out themselves, or they can hire Indian hide-skinners to do it.

"The main thing a white hunter will want is the buffalo head to hang on his trophy wall. We will tell him there are several taxidermists right here on the rez who will prepare and mount the head. Then there is the buffalo hide. It's the hunter's hide; he paid for it. So, he can either take the hide home untreated, or he can pay one of our Northern Cheyenne women for a tanned hide. If the hunter does not want the hide from his buffalo, he can give it to a Cheyenne woman who will tan it and then sell it on the open market. As for the meat, if the Whiteman wants the meat, he can pay us to process the animal, package the meat, and freeze the packages. If the hunter doesn't want the meat, he can give it to the tribe and the cost of field dressing the buffalo will be waived. The meat will be used at our ceremonies. Any extra meat will be given to needy families."

"What does it take to make your dreams happen?"

"There are three problems. The first problem is that in our culture one must earn the right to be listened to. I have not yet earned that right, but I am working at it. The second problem is money. But if, like you say, some rich people will give us the funding for the book project, we will use the profit to buy the van. When the tour groups take off, we will use the profit from the tours to build our lodge. Once we have the lodge, we will get our college courses going and accredited. When the money from those three ventures rolls in, we will start the buffalo pasture."

"You have plausible solutions for the first two problems. What is the third problem?"

"Ah, the third problem. It's the big one."

"And it is?"

"Apathy."

"Apathy?"

"Yes, apathy. The Northern Cheyenne have made many attempts to travel the Whiteman's Road. Those attempts have mostly been futile. So, everyone has quit trying. They are apathetic. Apathy is hard to fight. It silently kills its victims.

"Wouldn't the tribal government be willing to take this on?"

"The tribal government would be the worst bunch to do it. Our tribal government is too political; it's dog-eat-dog. Though we will need the tribe's approval, this project will work best if it is set up as a non-profit corporation with a board of five unpaid directors, none of whom can be more closely related than second cousins."

As Sarah finished sharing her vision and her dreams, we started down the long hill into Lame Deer. Near the bottom of the hill, we saw a flock of meadowlarks sitting on a barbed-wire fence. Pointing to the birds, I remarked, "They're wasting time. On a nice day like this, they should be migrating south."

"Songbirds don't migrate during the day."

"Oh," I mocked. "Do you think they find their way in the dark?"

"Yes, they do."

"How do you know that?"

"The birds tell me."

"I see. Just like the coyotes, the birds talk to you."

"Okay, wise guy. Tonight, I will take you to a place and teach you a thing or two!"

"You've already taught me a thing or two after the sun has gone down, but if there is more to learn, I'm a willing student."

"Shut up!" she replied, feigning irritation, "When you get on a roll you can out-talk a lawyer, and that's nothing to be proud of."

It was well after sundown when we started down the grade that brought us into the Tongue River Valley. As we approached the school, Sarah turned north onto the Birney Road and drove until we came to the trail that led to the Fighting Bears' place. Turning off the car lights, she went but a little way toward Joe and Maggie's cabin and then turned left onto an even fainter trail. It led us to a hay meadow in the bend of the Tongue River. We drove across the meadow and stopped at the edge of the riverbank. Reaching into the back seat, Sarah grabbed a blanket and motioned for me to come with her. We walked about twenty yards to the north. When we reached a place where the grass was long and soft, Sarah spread out the blanket.

"Lie down," she whispered, "and listen for birds."

"Listen for birds?"

"Yes, listen to them talking to each other. We'll probably hear meadowlarks, possibly the ones we saw today. We'll hear the chirping of white-crowned sparrows, and maybe the soft tweeting of mountain bluebirds."

Ten minutes of listening brought only silence. "I don't hear any birds. Do you?"

"Patience."

We waited five more minutes without hearing anything, not even a coyote howl. Then, faint and far away, we heard chirping. The birds were coming upriver, but not via a direct path. Their chirping sounds traveled from one side of the river valley to the other. Gradually, the sound became more distinct, allowing us to visualize their flight path. The birds were flying from one cluster of trees to another, and they were in no hurry to get wherever they were going. Small bunches of them landed briefly. Tweeting more loudly than the rest, they then scurried to catch the ones who had forged ahead. Eventually, the birds passed so close that we could hear beating of their wings. Then it was silent, but not for long. Soon, another group of birds came up the river valley. They had stronger, deeper voices, somewhat like the caw of a crow. They did not meander up the valley but came roaring over our heads like fighter jets making a strafing run.

"Pinon Jays," Sarah explained.

Then it was again quiet. Fifteen minutes passed before we heard more chirping sounds coming from far down the river. "Sparrow larks," Sarah announced.

"Why do the birds call to each other?"

"Sometimes it's mothers, telling their young to keep up. Occasionally, she scolds an adolescent who thinks he knows a better way. The young birds report their anxieties to their fathers and ask for assurance. Most of them are mated birds. They are complimenting each other on the fine brood they raised this summer. A few are first-time lovers. They are enriching each other's lives by sharing the beauty of the trip."

"In other words, bird-to-bird talk. Nothing of news or importance to people."

"That's not true."

"What are they saying that is important to us?"

"This evening, the birds told me that Hoimaha, the spirit who controls winter, is still far in the north. The first snow will not come for at least a month. Until then, we will continue to have a beautiful fall."

"What did you hear in the bird calls that told you that?"

"It's not what I heard that told me that. It's what I didn't hear."

"And what didn't you hear?"

"Did you hear any high-flying geese?"

"No."

"That means it is still warm and fall-like a thousand miles to the north, so the geese have no reason to fly south. For the next several weeks the temperature down here will be above normal with a gentle breeze from the southwest."

"Interesting. Did you learn anything else?

"Yes. But if I told you those things and how I knew them, you'd eventually know almost as much as an Indian. Now that's a scary thought."

CHAPTER TWENTY-THREE

Dey is still fightin' Custer

"Learning is not compulsory. Neither is survival."

E. Edwards Deming

"Well, what did ya think of Busby?" Joe asked as I walked into the school Monday morning.

"The poverty in that town is depressing. How long do you think it will be until the Northern Cheyenne find their way out of it?"

"The way it's going, never"

"Why not?

"For starters, there's Mother's Day, the first Tuesday of every month. That's when the unwed mothers get their check from the government. The money is needed, and it helps a lot of people get by, but in the long run Mother's Day is a bad thing."

"How so?"

"In the old days, the family was the underpinning of the Northern Cheyenne's strength. The father provided for his family and protected it. The wife ran the lodge, cooked, and looked after the kids. The husband and the wife were a team, eh? They were a real family. Mother's Day has upended that. Nowadays, there aren't many families among the younger folks. It's just unwed mothers with a jobless, young male Indians hanging around like a cur dog looking for a handout. "Do you know what real happiness is?"

"I haven't given it much thought, Joe. So, tell me. What is real happiness?"

"Real happiness is getting up in the morning and having something to do that needs to be done. There isn't much real happiness on the rez cuz there ain't many jobs. The white folks have most of the jobs. Take the schools. Nearly all the teachers are White. Every summer a new building or two goes up on the rez, but who builds them? Whitemen. There is lots of road work on the rez every summer, but who drives the big cats, the graders, and the dump trucks? Whitemen drive them, that's who. The IHS [Indian Health Service] hires a fair number of doctors, nurses, lab people, and dentists. Who are they? More white people. Those jobs need to start going to the Cheyenne if there is ever gonna be happiness on the rez.

"There is another reason for the poverty. It's because they are still fightin' Custer."

"Still fighting Custer?"

"Oui, they sure enough killed him in 1876, but the Cheyenne are still fighting his memory, and that also keeps 'em poor."

"How is Custer's memory keeping the Northern Cheyenne poor?"

"When Custer came this way, he was coming to kill Indians, even women and children. A hundred years later, the government hasn't got it done, but most Indians think the government is still tryin' to kill them. Let me tell you about two doctors, a husband and a wife. They came to Belcourt from someplace back East to help the Indians. The doctors soon found out that many of the high school girls had clap and syphilis. So, the doctors went to the high school and got all the girls together for a big talk. They told the girls about the bad diseases they could get from unprotected sex. They then told the girls that to keep from getting' those bad diseases, they should make their boyfriends wear a rubber. Ya won't believe what happened next!"

At that, Joe stopped talking, compelling me to ask the obligatory question, "And what happened?"

"Before a month passed, the old women of the tribe had run the two doctors off the rez."

"You're kidding! Why did they run the doctors off?"

"The old women believed the government sent the two doctors to Belcourt to get the girls to do things so they so they won't make any more Indian babies. It's that kind of thinking that keeps the Cheyenne in poverty. Now enough jawin' about things neither one

of us can change. I have to fix a leaking faucet in the girls' bathroom, and you have windows to caulk."

When noon recess was over Monday, Lisa came in for our last
reading session of the day. That afternoon, we learned that a con-
tagious virus, 'hydrophobia,' was sweeping through the animals in
the area, wild and domestic alike. When the family's bull caught
hydrophobia, it treed several children and had to be shot.

At the end of the chapter, there were not many pages left. The
fate that awaited Old Yeller was obvious, and I worried how Lisa
would respond when Old Yeller died. After all, her mother had died
only a few months ago, making it likely Old Yeller's death would
rekindle Lisa's grief. There was enough tragedy in the little girl's
young life that she didn't need more. But having started us down
this road, there was no turning back.

Later that day, Sarah asked me how Lisa was progressing with
her reading. "Very nicely! She can read entire paragraphs from *Old
Yeller* with only a little help."

"Excellent. Bring the reading lessons to an end this Friday. Lisa
is ready to return full-time to her class."

Friday, after the noon recess, Lisa sat down for our last reading
time. There was only one chapter to read. I knew it would be about
the loyal dog's death and thought it would be best if Lisa did not
read about it but rather listened. It went something like this:

One evening, when the family was walking back to the house, a
rabid wolf attacked them. Before the wolf could bite anyone, Old
Yeller came to the family's rescue. After a terrible fight, the faithful dog drove off the wolf. The price Old Yeller paid for saving
the family was getting hydrophobia. Travis, the oldest boy, had to
shoot his faithful dog. But a neighbor girl gave the family a puppy,
a puppy that had been sired by Old Yeller. At the end of the book,
the family's attention turned to the puppy.

As the last page was turned and the last word was read, there
wasn't a tear in Lisa's eye. Perhaps that was because on the reservation life is lived close to nature, and children are not shielded from
death. To them, life and death are an endless loop in which death
often brings life. Death comes when a deer passes near the cabin

and Grandfather shoots it. The children watch as Grandfather slits the deer's throat, and they see the steam condense in the cold air as warm blood drains from the deer's throat into a bowl. That night, the youngest child, a frail little boy, is nourished by blood soup, completing the circle of life. When Death calls again, he comes for Grandmother and finds her sleeping in a bed that has been moved to be near the warmth of the cook stove. On the reservation, children know Death. They know Death by sight. They know Death by smell. They know Death by touch, and they do not fear him.

As the last sentence was read, I slowly, somewhat ceremoniously, closed the book. Lisa stood, gave me a hug, and went upstairs on light footsteps, surprisingly light considering she was taking a good deal of me with her.

CHAPTER TWENTY-FOUR

A Home Worth Dying For

"In all of us there is a hunger, marrow deep, to know our heritage—to know who we are and where we came from. Without this enriching knowledge, there is a hollow yearning."

Alex Haley

When school was dismissed on Friday, Sarah and I set off on a trip. As we departed Birney, I merely followed her directions. "Take the Birney Road. When we get to the highway, turn east."

Darkness had engulfed us when we reached Broadus. Ten miles past Broadus, Sarah gestured to a gravel road that led south along the Little Powder River. The road took us to Gillette, Wyoming. Sitting amid a sagebrush-covered prairie, the town lacked any apparent reason to exist. But Gillette brought us one good thing, pavement. We followed it east. We had been on the road for more than three hours. My eyelids were drooping.

"Want me to drive?" Sarah asked.

"Sure."

The humming of the tires quickly put me to sleep.

I was jarred awake by a bright sun that burst through the pickup's windshield Looking around, I saw we were parked on a vacant lot in a disappearing town. The name on the water tower read, HARRISON. But Harrison where?

Hearing me groan as I unfolded my cramped body, Sarah woke and lifted her head from its resting place on the steering wheel. After rubbing sleep from her eyes, she reached into her rucksack.

"Eat," she said, offering me a cold, baked potato. As I ate the potato, she drove us east. In twenty miles, we came to Fort Robinson, Nebraska.

Fort Robinson is not a town; it's a restored military fort. According to the plaque at the entrance, the U.S. Army built Fort Robinson in 1874 to serve as the supply point for the Red Cloud Indian Agency, located a few miles farther down the White River. It was also the garrison for the army troops assigned to holding in check an Indian agency of several thousand somewhat hostile and always volatile Sioux. With the passing years, Fort Robinson's mission was modified to accommodate the army's needs in a changing world. It served as a remount station during World War I, building up one of the finest herds of Morgan horses in the world. During World War II, Fort Robinson was the site for K-9 training and a prisoner of war camp for German soldiers. When the war ended, the U.S. Army had no further use for Fort Robinson and sold the fort, the buildings, and twenty-two thousand acres to the State of Nebraska for one dollar.

Fort Robinson is laid out on an incline that gently slopes to the south, ending at the White River. To the immediate north, chalk-colored bluffs rise above the fort. A horseshoe-shaped road with a south opening defines the northern edge of the fort and creates a parade ground. A frame house occupies the middle of the parade ground. At one time the building was the home of the fort's commanding officer. But now, it's the administrative office for the Fort Robinson Park Service.

After making a counterclockwise drive around the parade ground, Sarah drove to the lower end of the historic fort and parked along some building-sized, shallow depressions. "Come," she said, getting out of the pickup. Walking to the middle of the closest depression, she sat down on closely cut, green grass. That faraway look, the kind that sees things in the long ago, appeared in her eyes.

"What happened here?" I reverently asked.

"By the spring of 1877, it was apparent we could no longer live in the Powder River Country. Despite the promises made to us in the Treaty of 1868, we had to leave our traditional home. Morning Star and Little Wolf brought their people to Red Cloud's Agency, only a few miles northeast of here. We were satisfied to join our Lakota friends. Red Cloud, Big Road, and Young Man Afraid of His Horses were there. It was reassuring to be among them. But soon, General Crook, the soldier chief in charge of Fort Robinson, told us that we must go to the Indian Territory, located in what is now Oklahoma. Having heard that the Indian Territory is dry, barren, and windblown, Morning Star told Crook we did not want to go, but the soldier chief said there are no rations for us at the Red Cloud Agency; we could not stay. When we protested, Crook promised that if we went to the Indian Territory and did not like it, we could return. We went to take a look.

"Things were terrible there. There was no game to hunt, and the rations were meager. The soil was poor, and there was too little rain to grow gardens. Most everyone got sick. Many died. After being at the Darlington Agency one year, we recalled the words of our elders when the Northern Cheyenne first came to the Powder River Country: It is better to die defending a beautiful place than to live to be an old man someplace else. We were someplace else, and we were dying. We longed for the Powder River Country where the air is cool in the summer and scented with the fragrance of the sacred white sage; where the waters of the Yellowstone, the Tongue, and the Powder Rivers flow clean and refreshing; where elk, antelope, deer, and buffalo graze on the sun-brightened prairie; and where pine trees softly whisper to us from the heights of the Wolf Mountains. Most important of all, we wanted to be near Noah'wus, our Sacred Mountain.

"We remembered that General Crook had promised us that if we did not like things in the Indian Territory, we could come back and live at the Red Cloud Agency. We had seen the Indian Territory, and we didn't like it. We wanted to go back, but John Miles, the man in charge of Darlington Agency, wouldn't let us."

"What happened?"

"On the night of September 9, 1878, 284 Northern Cheyenne slipped out of their lodges and started for home, led by Little Wolf and Morning Star. But between us and home lay a thousand miles. The army immediately sent soldiers to hunt us down. We had only eighty-seven fighting men, counting boys so young they were barely strong enough to draw a bow. On the very first day, cavalry troops attacked us. But soldiers who fought for pay were no match against Cheyenne who fought for their lives. The soldiers retreated, and we traveled over the prairie like the wind, fast and quietly. The army loaded soldiers, horses, and supplies onto a train and whisked them through the night to the first set of railway tracks we had to cross. There, in the middle of Kansas, soldiers were waiting for us. But one morning they woke to find that we had passed by in the night, unseen. We traveled seventy miles a day, and we did this day after day.

"Eventually, we reached the Platte River and the next set of railroad tracks. Again, soldiers were waiting for us. We slipped by them and sneaked into the Sand Hills. The soldiers could not drag cannons and supply wagons across the endless miles of soft sand, and they quit chasing us. However, the sand also made our traveling hard. We rested.

"While resting, we talked about what to do. It was late October. Winter was coming. We had no buffalo hides for tepees, no robes for sleeping, and little food. Morning Star counseled that we should go to Red Cloud's agency and slip in among the lodges of the Lakota, who would hide us and feed us. Little Wolf saw it otherwise. He thought spies and half-breeds going back and forth between the Red Cloud Agency and Fort Robinson would soon learn the Northern Cheyenne had returned, and they'd inform the soldier chief, who would force us to go back to Indian Territory. Little Wolf had heard that the Cheyenne who had earlier gone into Fort Keogh were being treated well. He and his followers decided to join the Cheyenne at Fort Keogh. That night, Morning Star's band and Little Wolf's band camped apart. Before the sunrise, Little Wolf's band departed for the Tongue River."

As we sat on the grass, a green station wagon bearing the insignia FORT ROBINSON STATE PARK slowly snaked down the road. The vehicle crawled toward us like an irritated bear. Standing, I struck a submissive posture. "Sit!" Sarah said sternly. "We have a right to be here!"

As the station wagon came abreast, the park ranger looked us over, but the vehicle continued creeping along. After circling around us, the car crawled back to the administrative offices and stopped. A park ranger got out and went into the building.

"So, how did things work out for Morning Star?" I asked.

"He sent a messenger to Red Cloud to ask if the Oglala would take in the Cheyenne. In two days, the messenger came back with Red Cloud's reply. He thought there was no escaping the Whites and advised Morning Star to surrender to the soldier chief. They did. Their guns were taken away, and they were put in a barracks, this one," Sarah explained, gesturing to the depression in the ground where we were sitting. "At first, Morning Star's band was fed, given wood for the stove, and allowed to come and go around the fort. Then one day a telegram came for the soldier chief, telling him that the Cheyenne must go back to Indian Territory. Morning Star refused. What he told the soldier chief will forever be repeated in Cheyenne lodges. He said, 'All we ask is to be allowed to live, and to live in peace. We bowed to the will of the Great Father and went south. There, we found that a Cheyenne cannot live. So, we have come home. It is better to die fighting than it is to die of sickness and hunger. Tell the Great Father that if he tries to send us back, we will kill each other with our knives rather than return to Indian Territory.'

"Morning Star's words were sent over the telegraph line to the Great Father in Washington. In a few days, word came back: The Cheyenne had to go back. They refused. It now was January. Winter was upon the land. It was bitter cold. To force the Cheyenne to go back to Indian Territory, the soldier chief locked us in our barracks. He did not give us wood for our stoves or food for our stomachs. The soldier chief thought that when the Cheyenne got cold and hungry, we would submit. We huddled together for warmth and went without food for five days. On the fifth day the soldier chief ordered that Morning Star be brought to him. But Morning Star's people would not let him go see the soldier chief. Instead, they sent three headmen. The soldier chief told the three headmen that the Cheyenne must go back south. The men refused. They were put in chains and locked in the guardhouse. That caused a loud commotion. Hearing it, the Cheyenne in the barracks prepared to fight. They retrieved a few guns and knives hidden underneath the floorboards.

"That evening we broke out. It was mostly starved women and children. The weakest ones were the slowest. They were shot in the back as they ran toward the river. By morning, the survivors had traveled seventeen miles. Soldiers dogged them for six days, surrounding them each evening. But each time, the Cheyenne slipped away in the dead of night.

"The end came on January second. Again, the soldiers found us. We had only three bullets left. When the bullets were gone, the troops rushed up and looked down into the washout where the Cheyenne were huddled, defenseless. The soldiers fired a volley of shots at us and fell back. Three Cheyenne climbed out of the washout. One had an empty pistol. Two had knives. They charged the soldiers. Bullets from a dozen rifles killed them.

"Of the one hundred forty-nine Cheyenne that came into Fort Robinson and gave themselves up, sixty-four were dead. But six Cheyenne escaped and made it to the Lakota camp, where they were taken in. One of them was Morning Star. Seventy-eight Cheyenne were recaptured, but they were not sent back to Indian Territory. Rather, they were allowed to stay with Red Cloud at his agency. But they weren't happy there. That fall, 1879, a small party of Northern Cheyenne decided to flee the Pine Ridge Agency. Spotted Wolf led them northwest along the southern edge of the Black Hills and into Wyoming. They were going home.

"The Indian agent at Pine Ridge sent the captain of his Indian Police, Man Who Carries the Sword, and nine other Indian police after them. When the police caught up with the Cheyenne, Man Who Carries the Sword ordered them to come back to the agency. 'I will die first,' Spotted Wolf said as he opened his blanket and reached for his rifle. The Indian police shot and killed him. They then escorted the remaining Cheyenne back to the Pine Ridge Agency.

"Let's walk," Sarah said. I want to give this place a good looking over because I will never come here again. It's too painful."

It was November eighteenth, but surprisingly warm. The wind was not stirring. The grass was cut close for the winter. The buildings were neat and tidy. The setting was serene and pastoral. Only a small plaque, level with the ground and nearly inconspicuous, bore testimony to what the government and its army had done here to the Cheyenne. It was brief and written in small print.

We left Fort Robinson late that afternoon and started for home. We did not get far before encountering a cold front coming in from the northwest on a strong wind. Ahead was Hot Springs, a little town nestled tight against the Black Hills. "Tonight, I'd like a hot bath and a warm bed," Sarah declared.

In the middle of downtown was a motel standing on the edge of a babbling creek. I got a room, secured Sarah behind a locked door, and went back to the truckstop we had passed on the east end of town for a couple of hamburgers and chocolate malts. We ate, took baths, and went to bed.

Sunday morning, the sun was hidden by fog. Despite the gloomy weather, Sarah was in a good mood, making it seem safe for me to ask a question that might require her to talk about yet another tragedy. But I wanted to know. "So, what happened to Little Wolf?"

"Before Little Wolf and his band struck out for the Tongue River, he and his warriors stole some cavalry horses. With fresh mounts, they quickly swept northwest. They spent the winter at the headwaters of the Powder River. That spring, they surrendered to White Hat, an army officer. White Hat led them into Fort Keogh. Little Wolf and his band lived at Fort Keogh for many years. My grandmother was born there in 1880. In 1884, we were given our own reservation. As soon as we had a reservation, the Cheyenne started to come home, one band at a time. The first to come back were those who had gone to live with the Arapaho. In 1891, shortly after the Wounded Knee Massacre, the remnants of Morning Star's band living on the Pine Ridge Reservation were allowed to come home. Over the subsequent years, most of the Northern Cheyenne who remained behind in Indian Territory have come back. As The People said when we first came to the Powder River Country, 'This is a good land. It is worth fighting for.' Although many Cheyenne died along the way, we have come home. This time, we are here to stay!"

CHAPTER TWENTY-FIVE

My Brilliant Idea

What is the difference between an optimist and a pessimist?
The pessimist is better informed.

When the calendar rolled over to December, the land acknowledged the coming of the inevitable. The deciduous trees draped themselves in a drab-gray and held their stripped-bare limbs up in silent surrender to the snowline that was slowly, but resolutely, marching down the face of the Bighorns. The wind hustled snow-laden clouds across the sky. Winter was coming. It was only a matter of time. At school, every window had been caulked, and the coal bin had been filled. There was not enough work to keep Joe busy, let alone an assistant. I needed several cups of coffee in the morning to wash down my pangs of guilt brought on by knowing that come noon I'd be eating a lunch I hadn't earned. When school was out each day, Joe and Maggie departed, leaving Sarah and me to lock the doors. If the wind was not bitter, we used the light of the increasingly shorter days to take close-by walks and then return to school to eat the supper Maggie had conveniently left in the refrigerator. Before departing and going our separate ways, we always played a game of cribbage. Sarah usually won, but what can one expect when playing a game in which chance plays a large role in determining the outcome.

The relationship between Sarah and I was solid and becoming increasingly normalized with every passing day. Life was good. Yet, I was concerned because I knew this bliss was not sustainable. I could not be the school's assistant janitor for year after year while living in a tent pitched along Poker Jim Creek. Long-range stability was needed. But how to obtain it?

One night rendered sleepless from trying to think of a way to get our future on a solid, sustainable path, the solution came to me. It was so obvious, so eminently practical, and completely doable that I felt stupid for not discovering it sooner.

When the sun peeked its head over Poker Jim Peak the next morning, it peered down on a Whiteman sacrificing himself to the Gods of capitalism by taking a sponge bath out of a saucepan, shaving with cold water, and dressing in natty-looking casual. That done, I struck out for Lame Deer, the Indian village that housed the Tribal Offices, the Bureau of Indian Affairs, and the Indian Health Service, better known as the IHS.

After driving around Lame Deer to get a feel of the community, I stopped in front of the IHS Clinic. Straightening my tie, tucking in my shirt, and trying to exude confidence, I strode into the clinic. The waiting room was bursting at the seams with unopened cardboard boxes. No one was at the front desk. "Hello?" I called out.

Down the hall, a middle-aged Indian woman poked her head out of a room. "Can I help you?" she perfunctorily asked.

"Yes. I'm wondering if you are in need of a physician."

"Are you a doctor?" she asked. I nodded. "And you wanna work here? Well, take a seat," she said, moving an unopened cardboard box off a chair, "The clinic director will want to see you!" Judging from the secretary's reaction, the clinic was having difficulty attracting and holding physicians.

Thirty irritatingly long minutes passed before the secretary returned. "Fill these out," she instructed, handing me a stack of forms. It was tempting to tell her what she could do with them. After all, what competent physician would want to work in this disorganized, lackadaisical mausoleum of inertia? Well, I would. A position with the IHS clinic would guarantee me permanence in Sarah's world.

As the last form was completed and signed, a well-coifed, mixed-blood woman came into the room. Extending her hand, she introduced herself and added, "I'm the Director of the Clinic. Please come to my office."

"Would you like a cup of coffee, doctor?" she asked, gesturing for me to sit in the folding chair in front of her desk.

"No thanks."

"How can I help you?"

"I'm wondering whether you have an opening for a physician."

"We always welcome applications."

Disarmingly pleasant, the woman quickly soothed my recently acquired petulance by chatting at length with me on a wide range of topics. But she always skillfully guided the conversation back to its common thread—what was my training and experience? She seemed pleased with my answers. "You should know that IHS has housing for our professional staff, and it's convenient to the clinic," she said, gesturing over her shoulder toward the tract homes right behind the building. "The rent is nominal. So, tell me, doctor, why are you interested in working on the Northern Cheyenne Reservation?"

"Last fall, I used my vacation time to go on a road trip to the West. While on that road trip, I drove past the Birney Day School on the bank of the Tongue River. It was such a beautiful setting that I stopped to take it in. Well, I fell in love . . . with the country."

"You fell in love with the country?" she replied, her voice ladened with skepticism.

"Yes. It's so peaceful. It's free from noise, congestion, and pollution. It's quiet and serene. To me, that's beautiful."

"I see. Tell me, doctor, if you secured a position here, would you see yourself staying long?" Her raised eyebrows indicated my answer was particularly important.

"Yes. I'd stay for a good long time!"

"You would, would you?" she commented, apparently requesting that I seal that commitment with a pledge.

"Definitely."

"Well," she said abruptly, "thank you for your time, doctor. We'll give your application careful consideration." Standing, she extended her hand, bidding me to take my leave.

Driving back to the Birney Day School, I was euphoric. I'd soon have a roof over my head, a hot bath every evening, and a soft bed. More important, I'd be a thread in the fabric of the Northern Cheyenne Indian Reservation and solidly ensconced in Sarah's world.

As soon as my pickup pulled into the school driveway, Sarah came storming out the front door. Coming up to my pickup with her hands firmly planted on her hips, she snapped, "Where have you been?"

"I went to Lame Deer."

"And you didn't tell anyone!" she said angrily.

"I drove right by the school," I replied, thinking that was a sufficient explanation. After all, she always knew my comings and goings, and this one should have been obvious.

"You should have stopped and told someone you were going to Lame Deer. You had everyone here worried sick!"

"Worried? Did someone get hurt?"

"No. No one got hurt. That's not the point!"

"I'm missing something here. Why are you upset?"

"For months you have been coming into the school each morning as regular as clockwork. Then right out of the blue, you don't show up. And you don't bother telling anyone where you are going. You just go on your merry way, leaving us to worry about you."

"Worry about me?"

"Yes, worry about you! We worried about you all morning. When you didn't show up by lunchtime, we concluded that you were either hurt or sick. So, Joe and I drove out to your camp. On the way up the creek, we saw tire tracks coming down the gulch that had been laid down this morning. Looking at the tracks, Joe asked me if you'd said anything about leaving," Sarah said as tears welled in her eyes.

"And leave you? What would make you think such a stupid thing?"

"It was in my vision."

My face flushed red, and my jaw tightened. How long, I wondered, is this woman going to persist in believing a groundless piece of mysticism that was nothing more than a temporary thought-disorder intentionally induced by self-inflicted starvation and hypothermia.

Seeing that I was angry, Sarah changed the topic. "So," she asked, "what did you do in Lame Deer?"

"I applied for a job at the IHS Clinic, and the chances look good!"

"Did the director ask if you planned to stay long?"

"As a matter of fact, she did," I smugly replied.

"And what did you tell her?"

"I told her that there were many things about the Northern Cheyenne Reservation that I like, and I could see myself staying a long time."

"You'll never get the job," Sarah said, shaking her head as if I had done something stupid.

"Why do you say that?"

"The Northern Cheyenne are a proud people. We are struggling to get back control of the reservation from Whitemen. The director of IHS will never hire a Ve'ho'e who plans to make the reservation his home."

As the ensuing weeks passed, I often checked my mailbox at the Ashland Post Office. One time, there was a letter from my clinic wondering if I was interested in coming back to work. Another time, there was a letter from my sister, wanting to know if I'd be home for Christmas. However, I never got a letter from the Director of the IHS Clinic, not even a rejection.

CHAPTER TWENTY-SIX

The Meaning of Heritage

"The ground on which we stand is sacred ground. It is the blood of our ancestors."

Black Elk, Oglala Sioux

Early Saturday morning, Sarah, the Fighting Bears, and I met at the school. Sarah jumped into my pickup, and we followed the Fighting Bears up the Lame Deer Road. Reaching the plateau, we turned off on the same logging road Sarah and I had taken several weeks earlier. We were after firewood. Most families had already gathered the easy pickings, but it seemed the Fighting Bears had delayed getting their firewood until it was timely to include Sarah and me in the outing.

Joe was particular about his firewood. He wouldn't even look at the dead cottonwood trees along the Tongue River. "They are hard to split, burn cold, and leave lots of ashes. Now the ash tree burns good, but you have to clear away a lot a limbs to get to the heart of the tree. Me, I like pine. Not the pine the wind has blown over and left lyin' on the ground. It's already started to rot, and it ain't worth sawin'. I like the dead pine that's standin' straight and tall. It's waitin', it's wantin' to be my firewood."

After a bit of searching, Joe found a tall, dead pine that met his requirements. From the back of his pickup, he retrieved a six-foot long crosscut saw. Carrying it over to the base of the dead pine, he looked at me and said, "Grab an end."

"Joe, give me a little instruction here. This tool is new to me."

"It's easy," he said. "Let me pull the saw out of your hands, and then you pull it outta mine. Don't bear down when you're pulling it. Let the saw do the work."

No sooner was the tree felled than Maggie limbed it with a razor-sharp, double-bit axe. Sarah came behind her with a well-worn measuring stick to put a dab of yellow chalk on the tree trunk every sixteen inches. Joe and I set the crosscut on the first yellow mark and started sawing. Once we fell into the sawyer's rhythm, it was surprising how quickly the sharp crosscut sliced through the tree. By the time we got the tree sawed up, Maggie had located the next dead pine, and the sequence was repeated. When two trees were cut and loaded into Joe's pickup, it was time for lunch—beef sandwiches, buffalo-berry pie, and coffee.

After lunch, we cut up another tree, bringing the load on Joe's pickup to the top of the sideboards and adding so much weight that the back of his pickup was lowered a good four inches. By then, the sun was about to drop out of the sky. It was time to call it a day. Our little caravan headed for the Fighting Bears' log cabin. Upon arriving, the women went inside to fix supper while Joe and I unloaded the firewood.

Supper was hot and delicious. As Joe put down his fork, he said, "Good fixin's, Maggie. I'm as full as a tick."

That was the cue for Sarah and I to clear the dishes and wash them. When that chore was done, the four of us gathered around the kitchen table and played rummy by the soft light of a kerosene lamp.

The next morning, Sunday December 17, I again met the Fighting Bears and Sarah at the school at ten o'clock. Our objective was to get another load of firewood. It was late afternoon when we loaded the last piece of wood into Joe's pickup. As we did, Joe looked up and saw something that startled him. Pointing toward the northwest, he exclaimed, "Would ya look at that?"

Following the extension of Joe's arm, we saw a dark cloud that ominously stretched across the northwest horizon and draped a gunmetal-gray curtain clear to the ground.

"That's one monster of a storm!" Joe exclaimed. "It'll be about midnight when that brute comes poking around."

As Joe predicted, the storm arrived at midnight, and it arrived with eye-opening fury. The wind shook my canvas tent like a wolf shaking the life out of an innocent lamb. Overhead, the cottonwood tree creaked and groaned, and then it uttered a loud pop as a huge limb broke and crashed onto my tent, tearing its way inside. In the morning, I initially fretted about my demolished tent. But then I realized this dark cloud had a silver lining. I'd inform Sarah that my tent was destroyed, and her crazy Ve'ho'e needs a place to live for the winter. I'll tell her that we should move in together, and, if custom demands it, we'll get married. After all, it is time. Grinning like a Cheshire cat, I started for the school.

Walking into the basement, I looked in the kitchen and saw Maggie standing over the sink, washing apples. Before we could exchange greetings, she disappeared into the pantry. Dawn was cleaning a pan. Being painfully shy, she pretended not to see me. A teacher appeared at the top of the stairs and started down. Then, remembering something that needed her attention, she turned around and returned to her classroom. There was no sign of Joe.

Standing inside the door and taking everything in, it hit me. Maggie, Dawn, and the teacher had purposely avoided greeting me. I hurried into the janitor's workroom to find Joe to find out what was up. He wasn't there, but a dim light seeped under the door to the boiler room. I opened the door and heard feet shuffling back and forth behind the boiler. "Is something broken back there, Joe?" Reluctantly, Joe stepped into the light. His face was seared in pain. He tried to say something, but his lips only quivered.

"What's wrong, Joe?"

He slowly shook his head from side to side. "Something terrible happened last night"

"What happened?"

"The wind blew in a big Indian, a drunk one and a mean one. He didn't like what he found."

"What do you mean?"

"Oh God!" Joe said, as tears streamed down his face. "He beat her up real bad."

Taking the stairs two at a time, I rushed to find Sarah. She was sitting at her desk. Though she surely heard me coming, she did not look up and her long, black hair hung over her face. "Sarah!" I exclaimed. When she still did not look at me, I put my hand under her chin and tilted her head up, causing her hair to fall to the side. The entire left side of her face oozed blood and plasma. Her eye was swollen shut.

"I'll kill the son-of-a-bitch that did this," I shouted.

Putting her finger to my lips, she said, "Shush. You're disturbing the children." Standing, she took me by the hand and led me out the school's front door. When we were out of earshot of the children, I grabbed Sarah by her shoulders and again demanded to know who did this to her.

"There is much that I must tell you. Let's walk to the river." When we reached the riverbank, Sarah sat beside the trunk of an ancient, gnarled cottonwood tree and gestured for me to sit across from her. Taking my hands in hers and drawing them into her lap, she said, "There are some things you need to know. They weren't worth talking about before, but now they are important, and I'll tell you. When I was a junior in high school, we had a really good basketball team. The star player was Wohkpi-ain'-o, which means Gray Hawk. Every girl on the reservation was in love with him, and I was one of them.

"The following fall, Gray Hawk went away to a big college to play basketball. Instead of finding glory, he found the bottle. Snow was on the ground when he came slinking back home. But on the rez, he was still a basketball star. One day, Gray Hawk sent a friend of his to see my brother and give him a bottle of whisky and an old car. The next day, my brother, still drunk from the whiskey, sought out Gray Hawk and honored him by singing a special song. Gray Hawk giving my brother a car and my brother singing a special song to him meant that when I came back to the reservation, I'd become Gray Hawk's wife.

"Your brother gave you away for an old car?"

"That was how it was done in the old days. A suitor had his messenger bring horses to a girl's oldest brother. If the horses were accepted, the oldest brother went to the suitor and sang a song for him. That meant his sister would marry the suitor. But those days are long gone. I cannot be had for an old car!"

"So, we should get married and put an end to their stupid idea!"

"Unfortunately, we can't. Instead, you must go."

"I must go?" I shouted. "Why?"

Sarah turned her head down so that her long black hair covered her face. She looked at the ground and fell silent. Okay," I whispered. "I won't yell. But tell me why I must go.

"We have little time left. Listen. Listen carefully. Listen as if your life depends on hearing every word I say. If you stay, you'll be dead before the meadowlarks return next spring. I don't know how it will happen or who will do it, but someone will kill you."

"Why would someone kill me?"

"Because in the eyes of the traditionalists, you would be stealing a Cheyenne woman who was promised to another man, a Cheyenne man. If you were Cheyenne, we could sneak away in the dead of night and return in a year or two, and everything would be okay. But you're a Whiteman. The traditionalists do not like it when a Ve'ho'e marries a woman who carries good Cheyenne blood. If we stay together, someone will kill you."

"It's my life. I'll take that chance."

"If you stubbornly insist on staying, there is only one way I can keep you alive, and I'll do it!"

"What will you do?" I challenged, brimming with anger.

"From where the sun stands now, I will never talk to you again. If you walk into a room, I will walk out. If I see you from a distance, I'll go the other direction. My eyes will find you only so they can avoid you. I will have nothing to do with you tomorrow, the day after that, or forever. Seeing that I don't talk to you, no one else will, not even Joe. Eventually, you will leave. You'll leave bitter, but you'll leave alive. I'll settle for that."

"Then we must leave. Both of us, together. We can go right now, this minute."

"I'd love to go with you, but I can't."

"For Christ's sake," I replied with a raised voice, "what do you mean you can't? Give me one good reason why you can't go with me! If you can come up with a good reason, I'll go away. But if you can't find a reason or come up with a problem we can't solve, then we will leave together!"

Sarah drew my hand to her cheek to feel the warm tears running down her face. But her tears did not change my mind or give me a satisfactory answer.

"You can come with me," I pleaded. "We did well together in Salt Lake City. We can go back there. We can go anywhere."

"This is my home. This is where I must be buried when my time comes."

"And in the meantime, what about you and your safety from that mean bastard that beat you up?

"I'll go live with Joe and Maggie. If Gray Hawk even steps foot on their property, Maggie will shoot him. He's a drifter. When the green grass comes, the first warm breeze will blow him away. As for Maggie, she will make a wonderful Nes-ke-eehe."

"What's a Nes-ke-eehe, a bodyguard?"

"Yes," Sarah said as a bemused smile whisked across her face. "A Nes-ke-eehe is sort of a bodyguard."

"Sarah, you're not looking down the road. The rest of your life is ahead of you. I promise to do my utmost to give you a good, happy one."

"I know you would do everything in your power to do that, and I'd find happiness being with you. But eventually, I will die. When we die, our spirit remains. For all of eternity, my Cheyenne spirit would be unhappy and restless wandering around in a Whiteman's world, knowing it does not belong there. My ancestors died so that I could live and die in the most beautiful place in the world. To leave the Northern Cheyenne Reservation would be to dishonor them. I'd be turning my back on my heritage. I cannot leave my ancestral home."

Needing time to compose a rebuttal, I temporarily changed the subject. "You said that when you returned, you learned your brother had promised that you would marry Gray Hawk. Where were you?

"When I finished my junior year of high school, my teachers thought that since I read a lot, I should go to the Haskell Institute in Kansas. The government paid for it, so I went. At Haskell, they taught me to be a secretary. When I was almost ready to graduate and come back home, they gave me some tests, lots of tests. A few weeks later, my counselor told me that a college in the East wanted me to come to their school. I told the counselor I had no money. She said I wouldn't need any. Someone there was willing to pay for an Indian girl to come to their school. I stayed at Haskell that summer to earn some spending money. When fall came, I boarded an eastbound train."

"Where did you go?"

"It was a small college. You probably never heard of it.

"Maybe not but tell me anyway."

"It is called Dartmouth College."

"You went to Dartmouth!"

"You've heard of it?"

"Yes. I've heard of it! It's a great school. What did you study at Dartmouth?"

"I majored in mathematics and minored in physics."

"Mathematics and physics?" I gasped.

"Yes, they are so precise and ordered. I loved it."

"Go on. What happened at Dartmouth?"

"I was there for nearly four years. Everything was so new and exciting that I didn't think much about home. The first summer, I went with a study group to Switzerland. My trip was paid for. All I had to do was occasionally go to teas at the president's house and be nice to old ladies with long strings of pearls around their necks and big diamonds on their fingers. I think I met the woman who paid for me to go to college, for my clothes, my spending money, and my trips. She was a tall lady who said very few words but her eyes talked kindly to me. Anyway, the following summer a group of us went to Italy. The last summer we went to Egypt. Before I knew it, I was about to graduate. It was toward the end of April. I was studying in the library when my roommate came running up to me with a letter. She was running because I never got letters. So, she knew this letter had to be important.

"I looked at the writing on the envelope and knew that Maggie had written the address. But as soon as I touched the letter, I felt my grandmother's spirit. She didn't know how to write, but the words were hers:

My sweet Sarah,

My bones are getting cold.
When the bluebirds sing this summer, I will not hear
them. There are some things I want you to have.
When you finish your book learning and come back home
and see Mrs. Fighting Bear. She will have those things.

Much love,
Your grandmother, Nellie

"Clutching the letter, I rushed out of the library to find my advisor. I told her I had to go home because my grandmother was dying.

"Early the next morning, my advisor drove me to the airport. By late afternoon, I was in Billings. Still clutching my grandmother's letter, I hitchhiked to the Birney Road and then walked the last six miles to my grandmother's cabin, getting there just before sunrise. Carefully, I opened the door and quietly slipped into the dark house.

"'I'm in here, Niskone,' Grandmother called out from her bedroom.

"How did you know it was me?' I asked, taking her hand.

"'Last evening, the coyotes told me you were coming. I stayed awake all night waiting for you."

"I wanted to take my grandmother to a doctor, but she refused to leave the Tongue River Valley because she wanted to die in her own house, not in a Whiteman's hospital. I cared for my grandmother for the last two months of her life. During the time we had together, I learned much about her. She married at eighteen and had been married only a year when her husband, my grandfather, died when his horse fell with him, and he struck his head on a rock, killing him instantly. Grandmother said it wasn't until her husband died that she realized how completely and hopelessly she loved him. Lifting her nightgown, Grandmother showed me how, in her mourning, she cut her thighs to relieve her grief and to have scars that would always remind her that she had once loved deeply.

"When Grandfather died, my grandmother was carrying my

mother. But not being sure she was pregnant, she had not told her husband. I asked Grandmother if she regretted not telling him. Grandmother told me that she had only one regret. She regretted that when her husband was alive, she failed to get something from him for her medicine pouch. Without his spirit in her medicine pouch, her power was not as strong as it could have been.

"And now," Sarah said, "I will show my grandmother that I listened well. Lean forward." Taking her folding knife out of her jean pocket, she ran her fingers across my head. Collecting a lock of hair, she pulled it taut and cut it off. Producing a leather pouch from her jeans pocket, Sarah put the lock of my hair into her pouch. "There," she said, pulling tight the strings of the pouch, "my medicine bag is complete."

"I want a lock of your hair, too," I said.

"No."

"No? You just took a good chunk of mine. Why can't I have a lock of yours?"

"Silly Whiteman, sometimes you amaze me by the things you do not understand. You have been here. You have touched many things in the Tongue River Valley. Levi will always have a small white mark where you stitched up his forehead, and he will tell his children about the Whiteman who cared for him. You might not have noticed, but while Lisa was learning to read, you became the loving father she never had. She will never forget you. Even the deer that come by your camp in the evening have changed their ways. They now circle around your camp and walk along the creek's north bank on their way to water. For years to come, the deer will travel that new path. You have touched many things here, more than you know. Part of you will always be among us. A lock of your hair has earned a place in my medicine pouch."

"But that doesn't explain why I can't have a lock of yours."

"What would happen to the part of me that you would take? It would go places I've never been, places where I don't belong. Our mother, the earth, would not like that."

With a swift move, Sarah used her knife to make a small but deep cut on her arm. A rivulet of blood flowed out. She placed her finger in the blood and used her blood-wet finger to dab a red line that ran down my cheeks from each eye. "Maiyum will see that you are in mourning. In his compassion, he will give you the wisdom to leave and the courage not to look back."

I tried to talk, but only muted sounds came from my mouth. Sarah put a finger over my quivering lips, closing them. "The first hard-faced moon of my vision has set," she whispered. "It's time for you to go."

Nodding, I slowly rose to my feet. With tear-swollen eyes, I walked back to the school. I was nearly to my pickup when reason penetrated my numbness. "You fool!" a voice inside of me shouted. "You can't leave her. Go back. You must take her with you. Don't ask her to come with you, tell her! If you have to, pick her up and carry her away!"

I ran back to the river. Seeing the gnarled cottonwood tree, I looked for Sarah. But she was gone. Where we had been sitting, there was a pile of long, black hair. My eyes followed the path that led toward the riverbank, and they came upon Sarah's shirt. Her jeans were a few yards farther. Beyond them, standing on the edge of the riverbank, stood Sarah. Her back was toward me. She faced the sun, holding her arms up to it. All around her, the grass glistened red, red with blood that streamed down her legs from long, ugly gashes.

"Sweet Jesus," I whimpered. Paralyzed, I didn't know what to do. But Sarah's grieving spoke louder than her words. What seemed so right only a moment ago now seemed so wrong. I realized that, like her ancestors, Sarah was doing what she had to do to live in the land of the Northern Cheyenne. She had to stay. Her heritage compelled it.

When I got back to the school, it was time for recess. But the children were not outside playing, and Joe was not leaning against the foundation having a smoke. The basement door was shut. Every shade at every window was pulled down. No sound came from the building, making the schoolhouse look empty, abandoned, and lifeless.

I got in my pickup, started the engine, and gave it only enough gas to allow me to slip away quietly. I crossed over the Tongue River and drove east—a long way east.

Epilogue

Fifty-six years have passed since my pickup last rattled across the plank-covered Tongue River Bridge. In the years that intervened, work consumed me. I never found time to look for the right woman to marry, to have children, and to live, as the storybook version goes, happily ever after. In all those years, a day seldom passed that something didn't make me think of Sarah and wonder how her life had unfolded. Did she find a way to help her people? Did she find happiness and fulfillment?

Before death finds me, I would like to go back to the Northern Cheyenne Reservation if for no other reason than to look one last time into those dark-brown eyes that twinkled with intelligence, laughed with mischievousness, and mesmerized me.